DATE DUE

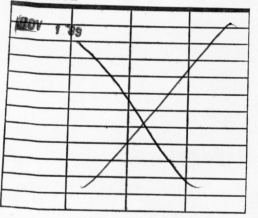

NOV 1 '89

Third World Voices for Children

Third World Voices for Children

Edited by
Robert E. McDowell and Edward Lavitt

Illustrated by Barbara Kohn Isaac

ODAKAI BOOKS
THE THIRD PRESS
JOSEPH OKPAKU PUBLISHING COMPANY, INC.
444 CENTRAL PARK WEST, NEW YORK, N.Y. 10025

Library of Congress Catalogue Card Number: 71-169091

SBN 89388-020-5

Printed in the U.S.A.

ODARKAI BOOKS, named after
the mother of the publisher of The
Third Press, is the Juvenile and Children's book imprint of The Third Press.

First Printing October, 1971
Second Printing June, 1972

For Judy and Marlene
and
Elizabeth, Rita, and Roy

And for Moses Ihonde

Contents

Africa

Introduction

A FRICA is a huge continent, three times the size of the United States. Across the continent live a great variety of black peoples who speak many languages, and who live in many different ways. South of the Sahara Desert there are over thirty nations of black Africans. From country to country, there are as many different ways of life as there are languages, and Africa has hundreds of different languages and dialects. Often one language group will be made up of no more than one million people. But language groups can be very large: in East Africa, for instance, over fifty million people speak Swahili.

The land of Africa is as varied as the people living there, with steamy hot areas along the equator, burning deserts such as the Kalahari in the south, vast rolling grasslands such as the South African veldts, soaring mountains in Tanzania and Kenya, and thickly grown rain forests such as those in the Congo.

From one end of the continent to the other for hundreds of years Africans have created excellent works of art such as wood carving, painting, pottery, textiles, basketry, tools, folklore, music, and literature. One of the best ways to learn about the lives of people is to study their art works and their literature. Of course, it is not possible to discover everything about Africa's three hundred million people in one book. But in the following stories, folktales, and poems, all written by Africans, we can learn many interesting things about their lives and thoughts.

Explanations of how the universe came into being differ around the world, yet they are always fascinating. The African story-teller explains quite beautifully in "How the Milky Way Came to Be" how part of the heavens came about. Such tales are told to demonstrate the power and beauty of nature; they are also man's attempts to explain the why and how of the universe. The single subject which most fascinates men all across Africa is creation.

Within this vast and complex universe not even the tiniest creature escapes man's curiosity, as we can see in the tale of Kwaku Ananse, the spider. West African people love Ananse stories and tell hundreds of different versions which portray the spider as a trickster. His boldness and bad behavior usually get him into trouble with the gods or the spirits. Sometimes in African spider tales Ananse is the winner of contests, though quite often he is punished for some evil-doing. In this case the story-teller might end by saying, ". . . and the spider is so ashamed of what he did that even to this day he hides away in the dark corners of the house."

Human beings are perhaps the greatest mystery of our earth. Certainly man is too complicated to be "manufactured" by the king's iron worker in "People Can't Be Made of Iron." This story also gives us a hint that unusual people can be the wisest among us—for in this tale the "madman" is intelligent enough to discourage the king in his foolish desire to make an iron man.

Even though men are flesh and blood, and not iron, they can be very strong and very brave as "Leopard Hunt" shows. "Leopard Hunt" is taken from the real story of the life of a royal West African who was born early in this century. At the beginning of his story, Prince Modupe says something which is all-important to most groups of people throughout Africa: "Our strength is in our togetherness." Yet, he also understands that there are some things that he must do on his own if he wants to grow up. In this story the proud youth goes into the bush alone to kill a wild animal in order to prove his manhood.

Prince Modupe's story took place many years ago. Perhaps not many boys along the Guinea Coast face wild animals alone these days to prove that they are men. In fact, many places that were just small towns in Africa when the prince was a boy have now grown into huge cities marked with skyscrapers. The world changes rapidly.

Rems Nna Umeasiegbu is worried that swiftly changing times in modern life will cause his people to forget all of their customs of the past. So that athletic contests, folk stories, and certain habits of politeness and respect practiced by the Ibo people of Nigeria will be remembered, Rems Nna Umeasiegbu has recorded them in a book entitled *The Way We Lived*. His descriptions of breaking a kola nut, burying an important man, and wrestling are selections from this book.

All over Africa, writers find it important to remember the past, and especially to think back over childhood. Camara Laye, for example, has warm memories of leaving his town to make a "Visit to the Village" of his grandmother in Guinea. It is interesting that the boy refers to the uncle who told him stories as they walked along, stories which he enjoyed though he had heard them a hundred times. Oral literature (that is, stories, proverbs, riddles, etc. which are told aloud) is the commonest kind of literature in Africa. Today, with more and more people learning to read, and with the increase in the number of books being printed, oral literature is disappearing. However, by writing down stories such as these, many Africans are helping to preserve some of the oral literature that might otherwise disappear.

You can also read here of Peter (Lee) Abrahams' pleasant boyhood memories of Joseph. Joseph proudly exclaims that he belongs to the Zulu tribe. Lee, who is Coloured (the word which is used in South Africa to describe people who have both black and white ancestors) is puzzled by Joseph. Lee is from a town and has no tribe to belong to. Joseph speaks only Zulu, while Lee speaks only Afrikaans (a language brought to South Africa by Dutch settlers). But the two boys soon learn a little of each other's language and develop a warm friendship as they play in the South African countryside.

One thing is probably the same with children all over the world—they wish for many things. As you can read in Philomena Kaka's poem, she would like to be an eagle, a traveling Hausa man (Hausa people live in northern Nigeria), or a queen so that she would not have to "go to school."

While there are about three hundred million people in all of Africa, the continent is so vast that people are much more widely scattered than they are in America. It is understandable, then, that most Africans live closer to nature than do most Americans. As you read through the stories, poems, and folklore from Africa, notice how often people speak of the weather, the landscape, the animals, and of nature in general.

Wrestling in Iboland

BY REMS NNA UMEASIEGBU

THROUGHOUT Iboland wrestling is an important sport. Young men have the chance to distinguish themselves and show their prowess. At times, disputes are settled with this all-important sport. An extremely popular girl who has had several approaches from suitors, may find it difficult to choose the man she will marry. What happens in this case, therefore, is that a wrestling competition is arranged for all the suitors and whoever emerges victorious marries the girl.

Inter-village wrestling competitions are not uncommon. Each village has its own wrestling ground, which is very soft and well looked after. The wrestlers are grouped according to their records of achievements. All the villagers are informed of any competitions, which usually come off in the evenings. A ring is made and spectators sit around this ring. The chief and titled men, the boys providing the music and the wrestlers sit inside the ring. Music is provided by boys who have been trained to produce this brand of music. The wrestlers squat and chat together. The competition is started by the two principal wrestlers from the two villages. Various techniques are employed and a wrestler can easily win the applause of the spectators with his adroit styles. Any competitor that is carried up—if his legs are no longer touching the ground—is declared defeated. Occasionally one competitor may be carried high up and thrown to the ground.

If it appears that no competitor is defeating the other, the wrestlers are said to be evenly matched. Another set of wrestlers comes in. Meanwhile, the boys are giving heart-stirring music, music that is capable of giving added strength to the weak. The total successes and failures of each team go to determine the result of the competition. The team that has the greatest number of successes becomes the winner and the chief presents the prize, which can take any form.

Breaking a Kola Nut

BY REMS NNA UMEASIEGBU

IN NIGERIA much importance is attached to kola nuts. If an Ibo man visits a fellow Ibo, he does not feel he is a welcome visitor until his host offers him kola. What normally happens is that the host shakes hands with his guests and ushers them to their seats. They talk generally for a few minutes before the host takes leave of them and enters his private room. He comes back with an old leather bag flung over his shoulder. The bag is opened and a piece of kola nut is brought out. Having touched it with his lips, the host hands it to the oldest man among his guests. The object of 'kissing' the kola nut is to prove to those present that he has given the kola in good faith and that it does not contain any poison, the argument being that if the nut does contain poison, the host will be the first to die. If he does not touch the kola with his lips, it will be rejected.

The oldest man then shows it to everyone present and each of them records his approval by touching the nut which is now being passed round. The oldest member of the team then breaks it saying as he cuts it in pieces:

'Live and let live; may we live long in order to see our great grandchildren.'

Those present respond by saying 'Amen.'

9

Another may join in with: 'He who brings kola brings life.'

The pieces of kola are passed round by the youngest among them; everyone partakes of it. Kola nut is always offered whether or not the host knows the guests are coming. In some places the youngest person breaks the kola instead of the oldest. In most parts of Awka, the duty falls on the oldest, but in Ngwaland, more often than not it is the responsibility of the youngest among them.

If palm wine is to be served, the youngest serves it. It is never served by the oldest. If the wine is being served by a member of the host's family, then such a person must drink a glassful first; if he does not drink he must sip it. If—on the other hand—it is poured out by one of the guests, the server hands a glassful to the host first. The object again is to make sure that it is harmless to drink. If there is a woman among them she drinks the wine kneeling down. If she is an elderly woman, say fifty years old, she drinks sitting down, like her male counterparts. On no account is wine ever served by a female. The last glass of wine is handed to the host. If the server makes a mistake about this, he is ordered to buy a gallon of wine as his punishment. The host either drinks the wine or gives it to the oldest man among them.

Burial of a Titled Man

BY REMS NNA UMEASIEGBU

THE TYPE of burial given to a dead man depends primarily on his social status when he was alive. Wealthy men, chiefs, titled men and warriors, are buried with pomp and pageantry, but poor and insignificant men without any incidents. As soon as a titled man falls ill, all the titled men in his area make a contribution which is given to his wives and children. This money is used in buying him things he wants. Medicine-men of renown are paid to take care of him. The titled man may fashion his own grave and order his own coffin, or he may give instructions to his children.

As soon as he dies, the Ukoro (a gigantic wooden drum whose sound can travel about ten miles) is beaten. An interval of at least ten minutes elapses before the next sound. This signifies the death of someone important. The villagers rush towards the direction of the sound. If the chief or titled man had been ill for a long time, the people will immediately know that he is now dead. Young men are sent to different villages in search of human heads. It is generally believed that a titled man or a chief must always be buried with human heads—otherwise he will not be given a rousing reception in the lower world. Young men are honoured and awarded titles if they are successful in bringing home these heads. Often too, they are given the privilege to choose any spinster in the whole village for a wife. In some parts of Iboland heads of animals are preferred to human heads, but places such as Bende Division and some parts of Ngwaland insist on human heads.

The corpse is washed, powdered and scented and dressed in a chieftain's regalia. It is placed on a well-decorated sofa. Two of his servants or slaves stand at the back of the sofa. Sympathizers are allowed to come in and pay their last respects. If he was a native doctor or medicine-man during his lifetime, his tools of trade are placed in the coffin. When the heads are brought, they are placed at each side of the coffin and the coffin is carried by four of his servants. He may be buried in front of his house or in one of his rooms, depending on the instructions he gave when he was alive. If he is buried in front of his house, a shrub is planted at the centre of the grave for remembrance sake. It is the eldest son of the family who first throws sand over the coffin. The crowd disperses to come back in four days' time for the waking and funeral ceremonies.

Joseph the Zulu

BY PETER ABRAHAMS

Each day I explored a little more of the river, going further up or down stream, extending the frontiers of my world. One day, going further downstream than I had been before, I came upon a boy. He was on the bank on the other side from me. We saw each other at the same time and stared. He was completely naked. He carried two finely carved sticks of equal size and shape, both about his own height. He was not light brown, like the other children of our location, but dark brown, almost black. I moved almost to the edge of the river. He called out in a strange language.

"Hello!" I shouted.

He called out again, and again I could not understand. I searched for a place with stones, then bounded across. I approached him slowly. As I drew near, he gripped his sticks more firmly. I stopped.

He spoke harshly, flung one stick on the ground at my feet, and held the other ready as though to fight.

"Don't want to fight," I said.

I reached out to pick up the stick and return it to him. He took a step forward and raised the one in his hand. I moved back quickly. He stepped back and pointed at the stick on the ground. I shook my head.

"Don't want to fight."

I pushed the stick towards him with my foot, ready to run at the first sign of attack. I showed my new, stubby teeth in a tentative smile. He said something that sounded less aggressive. I nodded, smiling more broadly. He relaxed, picked up the stick, and transferred both to his left hand. He smacked his chest.

"Joseph! Zulu!"

I smacked my own chest.

"Lee. . . ." But I didn't know what I was apart from that.

He held out his hand. We shook. His face lit up in a sunny smile. He said something and pointed downstream. Then he took my arm and led me down.

Far downstream, where the river skirted a hillside, hidden by a cluster of willows, we came on a large clear pool. Joseph flung his sticks on the ground and dived in. He shot through the water like a tadpole. He went down and came up. He shouted and beckoned me to come in. I undressed and went in more tentatively. Laughing, he pulled me under. I came up gasping and spluttering, my belly filled with water. He smacked me on the back and the water shot out of my mouth in a rush. When he realized I could not swim he became more careful. We spent the afternoon with Joseph teaching

me to swim. At home, that evening, I stood beside Aunt
Liza's washtub.

"Aunt Liza . . ."

"Yes?"

"What am I?"

"What are you talking about?"

"I met a boy at the river. He said he was Zulu."

She laughed.

"You are Coloured. There are three kinds of people: white
people, Coloured people, and black people. The white people come first, then the Coloured people, then the black
people."

"Why?"

"Because it is so."

Next day, when I met Joseph, I smacked my chest and
said:

"Lee! Coloured!"

He clapped his hands and laughed.

Joseph and I spent most of the long summer afternoons together. He learnt some Afrikaans from me; I learnt some
Zulu from him. Our days were full.

There was the river to explore. There were my swimming lessons, and others.

I learnt to fight with sticks; to weave a green hat of young willow wands and leaves; to catch frogs and tadpoles with my hands; to set a trap for the *springhaas;* to make the sounds of the river birds.

There was the hot sun to comfort us. . . .

There was the green grass to dry our bodies. . . .

There was the soft clay with which to build. . . .

There was the fine sand with which to fight. . . .

There were our giant grasshoppers to race. . . .

There were the locust swarms when the skies turned black and we caught them by the hundreds. . . .

There was the rare taste of crisp, brown baked, salted locusts. . . .

There was the voice of the wind in the willows. . . .

There was the voice of the heaven in thunderstorms. . . .

There were the voices of two children in laughter, ours. . . .

Visit to the Village

BY CAMARA LAYE

I OFTEN used to go and spend a few days at Tindican, a small village to the west of Kouroussa. My mother was born at Tindican, and her mother and brothers still lived there. I was always highly delighted to be going there, for they were very fond of me, and my grandmother in particular, for whom my visit was always a great treat, took great pleasure in petting me; and I for my part loved her with all my heart.

She was a tall woman, still with jet-black hair, slim, very erect, and strong; in fact, she was still fairly young and still did her share in the farm work, though her sons, who could cope with it all quite easily themselves, had often tried to make her give it up; but she would not hear of it, and obviously it was in this continual activity that the secret of her youthful vigour lay. She had lost her husband soon after their marriage, and I had never known him. Sometimes she would talk to me about him, but never for very long; almost at once, her voice would be choked by tears, and so I know next to nothing about my grandfather, and I was unable to picture him in my mind's eye, for neither my mother nor my uncles would talk to me about him: in our land, we hardly ever speak about dead people whom we have loved very much; we feel too sick at heart when we remember them.

Whenever I went to Tindican, it was always with my youngest uncle, who used to come to fetch me. He was younger than my mother and was not much more than an adolescent; and so I used to feel that he was still very close to my own age. He was very good-natured, and my mother did not have to tell him to look after me; he was naturally kind, and needed no telling. He would take me by the hand, and I would walk beside him; he, out of consideration for my extreme youth, would take much smaller steps, so that instead of taking two hours to reach Tindican, we would often take at least four. But I scarcely used to notice how long we were on the road, for there were all kinds of wonderful things to entertain us.

I say "wonderful things," because Kouroussa is quite a large town and the life of the country-side and the fields is lost to us; and for a town child, such life is always wonderful. As we wandered along the road, we would startle out of their hiding-places here a hare, there a wild boar, and birds would

suddenly rise up with a great rattle of wings; sometimes, too, we would encounter a band of monkeys; and always I would feel a little shock of fright in my heart, as if I myself were more startled than the wild creature that had been warned by our approach. Observing my rapturous delight, my uncle would collect pebbles and throw them far in front of us, or would beat the tall grasses with a dead branch, the better to stir up the game. I used to imitate him, but never for very long: in the afternoon, the sun burns fiercely down upon the savannah; and I would soon come back to him and slip my hand into my uncle's. And we would wander quietly along again.

"I hope you're not feeling too tired?" my uncle would ask.

"No."

"We can have a little rest, if you like."

He would choose a tree—a kapok tree or any tree that gave a sufficiency of shade—and we would sit down. He would tell me the latest news about the farm: calvings, the purchase of an ox, the clearing of land for a new field or the misdemeanours of a wild boar; but it was the births in particular that excited my interest.

"One of the cows has calved," he would say.

"Which one?" I would ask, for I knew each animal by name.

"The white one."

"The one with horns like the crescent moon?"

"That's the one."

"And what sort of calf is it?"

"A fine one, with a white star on his forehead."

"A star?"

"Yes, a star."

And for a little while I would think about that star, I would see it in my mind's eye. A calf with a star on his forehead: that meant he was to be the leader of the herd.

"Oh, but he must be beautiful!" I would say.

"You can't imagine anything so beautiful. His ears are so rosy, you'd almost think they were transparent."

"I want to see him at once. Shall we go and see him as soon as ever we arrive?"

"Of course."

"You'll come with me, won't you?"

"I'll come with you, you little scare-cat."

Yes, I was scared of all big animals with horns. My little playmates in Tindican used to go up to them without the

slightest fear, hanging on their horns and even jumping on their backs; but I used to keep my distance. Whenever I had to go off into the bush with a drove of cattle, I would watch them grazing, but I would never go too close to them; I liked them, but I was afraid of their horns. Of course the calves had no horns, but they made sudden, unexpected movements: you couldn't really trust them.

"Come on!" I would say to my uncle. "We've lain here long enough."

I was impatient to get there. If the calf was in the paddock I would be able to stroke him: in the paddock, the calves were always quiet. I would put a little salt on the palm of my hand, and the calf would come and lick the salt; I would feel his tongue gently scraping my palm.

"Let's hurry!" I would cry.

But my legs weren't used to such haste, and I would soon

slow down. And we would saunter along, walking as slowly as we liked. My uncle would tell me how the monkey had foiled the panther when it wanted to eat him up, or how the palm-squirrel had kept the hyena waiting all night long for nothing. These were stories I had heard a hundred times, but each time I heard them with renewed pleasure; my laughter used to send up the game all round us.

Before we even reached the outskirts of Tindican, I would see my grandmother coming to meet us. I would drop my uncle's hand and run shouting towards her. She would lift me high in the air, then press me to her bosom, and I used to squeeze her as hard as I could, flinging my arms around her, overcome with happiness.

"How are you, my little man?" she would say.

"I'm fine!" I would cry.

"Now, is that so?"

And she would look me over, feeling me; she would look and see if my cheeks were fat, and she would feel me to see if I was something more than just skin and bones. If she was satisfied in her investigations, she would congratulate me; but if her fingers felt only skin and bone—for I grew very fast, and that made me thin—she would groan.

"Just look at that!" she would say. "Don't they give you anything to eat in town? You're not going back until you've put some flesh on these bones. D'you hear me?"

"Yes, Grandmamma."

"And how are your mother and father and everybody at your place? Are they all well?"

And before she would set me down again, she would wait until I'd told her all the news about everyone at home.

"I hope the journey hasn't worn him out," she would say to my uncle.

"Not at all," he would reply. "We've been crawling along like tortoises, and now he's ready to run like a hare."

Then, more or less reassured, she would take my hand, and we would walk to the village, and with my hands in theirs we would all—my granny, my uncle and myself—make our entry into the village. As soon as we reached the first huts, my grandmother would shout out:

"Folks, here's my little man just arrived!"

The women would come out of their huts and run towards us, exclaiming and laughing:

"Why, he's a real little man! That's a real fine little man you've got there!"

Many of them would lift me up to press me to their bosoms. They, too, would carefully examine my appearance—how I was looking and what clothes I was wearing, for they were town clothes, and they had to declare that everything was splendid, and said that my grandmother was very lucky to have a fine little man like me. They came running from all over to greet me; as if the head of the canton in person had come to Tindican; and my grandmother would be glowing with pride and joy.

Stopped like this at every hut, acknowledging the enthusiasm of the village women and giving everyone news of my parents, it used to take at least two hours to make our way over the two hundred yards or so that divided my grandmother's hut from the first huts in the village. And when these good ladies finally did leave us, it would be to supervise the cooking of enormous plates of rice and dishes of chicken which they were to bring us for the festive dinner in the evening.

How the Milky Way Came to Be

Up there, in the sky, there are billions of stars. No one knows how many, because no one can count them. And to think that among them is a bright road which is made of wood ashes,—nothing else!

Long ago, the sky was pitch black at night, but people learned in time to make fires to light up the darkness.

One night, a young girl, who sat warming herself by a wood fire, played with the ashes. She took the ashes in her hands and threw them up to see how pretty they were when they floated in the air. And as they floated away, she put more wood on the fire and stirred it with a stick. Bright sparks flew everywhere and wafted high, high into the night. They hung in the air and made a bright road across the sky, looking like silver and diamonds.

And there the road is to this day. Some people call it the Milky Way; some call it the Stars' Road, but no matter what you call it, it is the path made by a young girl many, many years ago, who threw the bright sparks of her fire high up into the sky to make a road in the darkness.

Nyangara, the Python

ONCE UPON a time there was a Chief who had, as his Medical Adviser, a Python, whose name was Nyangara.

Now one day this Chief fell very sick indeed, so he called the men of his village together and he said, "My men, I am very sick . . . and I fear . . . I may die . . . if I do not see . . . my Doctor. Go up . . . all of you . . . to the cave . . . on the top of the hill . . . where my Python lives . . . my Doctor . . . Nyangara. And sing him . . . the magic song . . . which you know . . . Then he will come . . . out of his cave . . . and you will bring him . . . to me. When you go . . . take him a pot of beer . . . as a present . . . from me." So the men did as they were told. They climbed up to the top of the hill, stood outside the cave of Nyangara the Python, and sang him the magic song. But when he uncoiled two, three, four coils, the men were so frightened that they dropped the pot of beer, and they ran away.

Then they went back to the Chief and said,

"We are very sorry Chief, but you will have to die without your Doctor, as we are too frightened to bring him to you."

Now the Chief was very sad indeed that no one was brave enough to bring him his Python.

But the little children of the village heard what the men had done, and they said,

"Let *us* go up the hill to fetch Nyangara the Python, the Chief's Doctor."

So they went to the Chief and they said,

"Father, let *us* go up the hill to fetch your Doctor."

And the Chief said,

"Thank you . . . my children. I will teach you . . . the magic song . . . which you must sing . . . outside the cave . . . of Nyangara." So he taught them the song, and he said,

"Now . . . my children . . . you must take . . . another pot of beer . . . to my Doctor . . . as a present . . . from me."

So, twenty little children took the pot of beer and set off. Up, up, up they climbed, right up to the top of the hill and they stood in a row outside the cave of the Python and began to sing,

"Nai-we Nyangaya-we,
Ta zo ku wona, Nyangaya.

Nai-we Nyangaya-we,
Mambo wedu wofa, Nyan-
gaya.

Nyangara chena, Nyangara
chena."

"Please, please, Nyangara-we,
We want to see you Nyangara.

Please, please, Nyanagara-we,
Our Chief is dying, Nyangara.

Nyangara come out,
Nyangara come out."

And the Python answered them from within, saying,

"Ai-wa wana washe

Hii-hai-ha, Kwire chinyere.
Wamwe wakawiya pano.

Zuru riya ha-ya, Kwire chinyere.
Waputsa pfuko wedoro

Hii-hai-ha. Kwire chinyere."

"Yes, yes, children of the
Chief,
Climb up here.
Others came here only yester-
day,
Ha-a-ia, climb up here.

They broke the pot of beer
and ran away.
Are *you* going to run away?"

But the children stood stock still and went on singing.

"Nai-we Nyangaya-we,
Ta zo ku wona, Nyangaya."

"Please, please Nyangara-we,
We want to see you Nyan-
gara."

And then the Python began to uncoil himself and come out of the cave. He uncoiled three . . . four . . . six . . . seven . . . nine, all ten coils, and came right out of his cave. Then he curled himself up onto the shoulders of nineteen little children, and the twentieth walked in front with the pot of beer on his head, out of which the Python drank as they went along.

So they brought him down, down the hill to the Chief's hut. And they put him down outside the door. They opened the door and looked inside, and there was the Chief, lying on his mat, and he was very sick indeed.

Then the Python went inside the hut and they shut the door after him.

So Nyangara the Python set about the Chief at once. He licked him all over his back, down his legs, up his front, and all over his face; and when he had finished licking his face, the Chief woke up, quite well again, and he said,

"Thank you, my Python, for coming to see me. Now I'll send you back to your home in the cave."

So he called the little children and said,

"Take my Python, my Nyangara, back to his cave on top of the hill, and when you go, take him an ox as a present from me."

So the little children took Nyangara back to his cave. And when they came back, the Chief said,

"Now, my children, you can take another ox for yourselves, and have a feast of meat. But don't you let the grownups have any, for *they* would have let me die."

People Can't Be Made from Iron

A VERY LONG TIME AGO there was a king who called Walukaga, chief of his smiths, and gave him a great quantity of iron and said, "I want you to make a real man for me, one who can walk and talk, and who has blood in his body, and who has brains."

Walukaga took the iron and went home, but he was at a loss what to do, and no one could advise him how to set about making the real man. He went about among his friends telling them what the king had said, and asked what he had better do. No one was able to give him any advice. They all knew that the king would not accept anything short of an honest trial, and would punish the man for not carrying out his commands.

On the way home one day Walukaga met a former friend who had gone mad, and who lived alone on some wasteland. Walukaga did not know that he was mad until he met him. When they approached each other, Walukaga greeted his old friend, and the madman asked him where he had come from. Walukaga reasoned for a moment and then said to himself, "Why should I not tell him my story? Even though he is mad, he used to be my friend." So he answered, "I have come from some friends where I have been trying to get advice."

The madman asked what advice he wanted, and Walukaga

told him all the king had said, and about the work he had given him to do, and how he had given him the iron, and then added, "What am I to do?"

The madman answered, "If the king has told you to do this work, go to him and say that, if he really wishes to have a nice man forged, he is to order all the people to shave their heads and burn the hair until they have made up a thousand loads of charcoal, and he is to get one hundred large pots of water from the tears of the people with which to slake the fire and keep it from burning too fiercely."

Walukaga returned to the king and said to him, "My lord, if you wish me to make this man quickly and well, order the people to shave their heads and burn their hair, and make a thousand loads of charcoal out of it for me to work the iron into the man. Further, make them collect a hundred pots full of tears to act as water for the work, because the charcoal from wood and the ordinary water from wells are of no use for forging a man."

The king agreed to the request and gave the order to all the people to shave their heads and burn their hair into charcoal, and to collect all the tears. When they had all shaved their heads and burnt their hair, there was scarcely one load of charcoal, and when they had collected all the tears there were not two pots full of water.

When the king saw the results of his endeavours, he sent for the smith Walukaga and said to him, "Don't trouble to make the man, because I am unable to get the charcoal or the tears for the water."

Walukaga knelt down and thanked the king. He then added, "My lord, it was because I knew you would be unable to get the hair for charcoal and the tears for the water that I asked for them; you had asked me to do an impossible thing."

All the people present laughed and said, "Walukaga speaks the truth."

Why the Spider Has a Small Head

THEY SAY that once a great hunger came, and that Kwaku Ananse, the spider, said he would go and search for meat and vegetable food and bring it that he and his wife Aso might eat. He went into a certain stream and there he met certain people. Now these people whom he met, excuse my saying so, were spirits. When Ananse met the spirits, they were standing in the water and splashing the stream-bed dry to catch the fish. Kwaku Ananse said, "Brothers, may I come and splash a little too?"

The spirits said, "Come."

Ananse went, and he saw that they were using their skulls to splash the stream dry. The spirits said to Ananase, "You have seen that which we take to splash the stream dry. Will you allow us to remove your skull in order that you may splash too?" Ananse said, "I will permit you, take it off for me."

Of a truth, the spirits removed it and gave it to him. Kwaku Ananse and the spirits joined together in splashing the bed of the stream dry. As they splashed, the spirits raised a song:

"*We, the spirits, when we splash the river-bed*
  dry to catch fish, we use our heads to splash the water.
O the spirits, we are splashing the water."

31

The spider said, "This song is sweet, may I sing some of it?" The spirits said, "Sing some." And he lifted up his voice:

"The spirits, we are splashing the water,
    we take our heads to splash the water.
O the spirits, we are splashing the water.
Since the Creator made things,
    do we take our heads to splash the water?
O the spirits, we are splashing the water.
I take my head to splash the water dry today O,
    O the spirits, we are splashing the water."

Ananse finished singing, and the spirits told him, saying, "We have splashed, we have got fish, your share is a basketful. Take it and go and eat. Take your skull, join it on your body, and go off. But what we have to say most particularly is this—the very day you sing any of that song, your skull will open and fall off."

The spider said, "Fish in abundance, which you have given to me, is all that I desire, and as for a song—for what reason should I sing it?"

The spirits said, "That is well, go off."

So the spider set off. The spirits, too, got everything to-

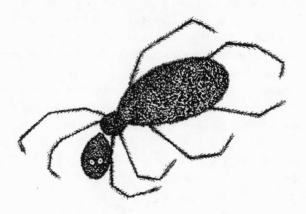

gether and they, also, went away. When the spirits had reached yonder, as it were, then they raised their song:

> "We, the spirits, when we splash the river-bed dry
> to catch fish, we use our heads to splash the water.
> O the spirits, we are splashing the water."

And the spider heard the song and he, too, took it up:

> "Since the Creator made things
> have we taken our heads to splash the water?
> O the spirits, we are splashing the water."

No sooner had he finished than his skull opened and dropped off. Ananse lifted it up and held it against his chest. He said, "Spirits, spirits, my head has fallen off."

The spirits heard, and they said, "That's the spider. He hasn't listened to what we told him, and he is calling us. Let us all go back and hear him."

Almost immediately, Spider came hastening along. He said, "*Puo!* Children of my father! My head has opened and fallen off, so I beg of you, if I have done you any harm, forgive it. You are in the right, but take my head and put it back in its place for me."

The spirits took it, and replaced it. They said to him, "Now, if you sing this song again and your head falls off again, we shall not answer when you call us. So get along with you!" The spirits set off again.

As they were going they sang their song. Then Ananse began to sing again, and his head became detached and fell off, *kutukum!* Again he lifted his head and clapped it against his body. He leaped to the side of the path. *Sora!* was the sound of the grass parting as he entered it. "Path, save me!" he said. "When the day dawns that I become rich, I shall share my riches with you."

Path opened up and hid Ananse in the tall grass along its side. Now he was safe from the spirits forever.

That is why, whenever you see Kwaku Ananse, the spider, you see him with a small head and a very big body.

Leopard Hunt

BY PRINCE MODUPE

WHEN LIGHT flooded the tops of the trees, Lamina's hand pressed heavily on my shoulder. He was looking at me but saying nothing. I wanted him to say something. I wondered whether he would camp on the spot and wait for me to emerge from the forest. Or would he go back to the village? I hoped he would wait but I did not want to ask him to do it. Lamina's hand pressed deeper into my shoulder. He felt my muscles, nodded his head in approval. He redipped my arrows and the tip of my *fange* sword into the poison. I was armed with all any man should need.

I passed through the clinging screen of matted creepers ahead of the daylight. The enormous boles of the tree trunks were only a little darker than the spaces between them. I thought about leopards, hoping the power of my thought would bring one to me. This was the hour when they look for resting places after a night of prowling and killing. Often the rest place is a cave. But I knew of no such cave in this forest, only that the whole jungle seemed an enormous cave, roofed with darkness. The smell of the forest was cave-damp. Under my bare feet was moss. I longed for dry brittle things —twigs snapping in the fire of my mother's kitchen, a grass sleeping mat under my body, thatch rustling on a roof above my head.

I stood quietly on the moss, trying to let myself be filled with the feel of the forest. I had food with me for three days, but I hoped I would not have to stay that long. My stomach could hold out for three sundowns but I was not sure about my courage. A leopard who finds himself at daybreak some distance from his lair usually takes his day's rest on a tree limb. This gives him a lookout position from which he can pounce on anyone or anything passing below. Many leopards lived in this jungle; we had the pelts of many who had died in this bush. I felt that death might be waiting for me above my head in any tree.

I pressed on deeper into the forest along a narrow trail, making silent talk of encouragement to myself. My eyes ached with the great effort of trying to watch for danger above me, all around me. Part of the terror was that of being alone. Africans conduct most of their activities in groups. We are not a solitary people. Our strength is in our togetherness.

After a while the thought came to me that instead of walking about aimlessly and exposing myself to the unseen, I would do better to find the evening watering place of the forest animals and conceal myself.

I felt better as soon as I had decided to become the hidden aggressor myself instead of waiting for death to drop down upon me from every overhanging limb. I made myself interested in the slope of the land, such slope as there was. I was still wary but I was over the paralysis of sheer panic. Not every twisted liana was a python waiting to crush me in its coils. Not every rustle hidden by trees was a devourer. I found a small ravine and worked my way down its slopes.

The ravine ended as I hoped it would in a small clear stream cutting through the forest. The relief of seeing bright sunlight sparkling on water was exhilarating after the massed

gloom of the forest. The very odor of the jungle is the odor
of death—the rotting vegetation, the sickish sweet masses of
fungi, the overheavy perfume of blossom on vines which
have worked their way up above the crown of the trees. The
thump of a falling seed pod is loud as a crack of thunder in
this vast silence. The mass of the growth, the extravagance of
vegetation belittles man, shrinks him to grub size. That is
perhaps the real terror of jungle, more frightening than the
tooth and claw hazards, although they, too, are awesome.

Along the bank of the stream I found a shelter which had
been formed in flood stage, an undercut bank. In it I was
protected from above, behind, and beneath me. I could at
least see what approached, if any danger stalked me.

In the clay where an animal run entered the stream, I saw
that the feet of many animals had brought them here to
drink. Much as I wanted to see the tracks to know what animals had made them, I resisted because there must be no
man-smell to keep them away at dusk. I tested the wind with
a clod, crumbled to dust. I was downwind from the watering
hole.

It was past midday when I had located my waiting spot.
Not too long to wait before the silent forest would come

alive. I began to notice details around me. A fallen giant of a
tree lay out over the water and a great mass of debris had
lodged in the branches. A red and blue lizard whose skin was
bright as beads slithered over the trunk. I lost sight of him
but soon a great monitor lizard as long as I was tall crept into
sight, then lay absolutely quiet, waiting, as I thought, for a
waterfowl to perch within his reach. He was screened from
above by the foliage of a still-green branch, and from where
I sat he seemed nothing more than a sun-dappled swelling on
the trunk. He must have seemed nothing more than that to
the red-footed webbed creature who became his victim. A
whole pageant of small animal life passed before me during
the afternoon. Strange as it may seem, I even dozed a few minutes. The heat was relaxing and I felt reasonably secure.
My one great fear was not of the animal I hoped to get at
evening, but that I would have to spend the night alone in
this spot.

I know now that the terrible sounds which come out of the
jungle at night are made by animals, creatures like the tree
hyraxes and pottos, but even our cleverest hunters believed
that the unearthly, skin-chilling night sounds of the forest
were made by malevolent spirits. There is no hiding place
against demons, the nightmarish creatures of imagination. As
for the actual, the four-footed dangers, even a hyena is brave
at night. There was a considerable growth of reeds along the

banks of the stream and this I saw as a good sign for my purposes. It was the kind of growth where a leopard would skulk
waiting for game to pass. I began to think of the leopard I
hoped to see as a sort of release from the horror of having to
spend the night by the river.

The first large creatures I saw at the water hole were a pair
of red river hogs. They were so close to me I could see the
coarse texture of their bright red-orange bristles, the white
tufts at the ends of the ears. They drank, muddied the water,
passed on to the other side of the stream. No rustle in the
reeds as yet.

A little water chevrotan drank daintily a bit upstream
from the hogs and took to the water keeping only his nose
above the surface. He would have been easy prey for a waiting leopard, I thought, but there was scarcely a breeze-ripple
in the reeds. Monkeys, little grey colobus creatures, swung
out on branches overhanging the water. There was a great
troop of them and they seemed to be having a nasty family
palaver of some sort which none of them could settle.

Fruit-eating bats darted in and around the monkeys making weird cries from their monstrous fleshy lips.

I saw none of the omen-birds, no sign was given me of what I might expect at any moment.

I watched a number of antelope nuzzling the water, shaking their heads, drinking, ears alert. There were several fawns in the group which the adults kept screened with their own bodies. They sensed lurking danger before I did, gave me the cue to tauten my bow. I could not get to my knees in the cramped spot I was in. Slowly, I eased forward; slowly, a bit at a time, changed from my left to my right knee. I could feel the satisfying flex of the bow in my hand. Not out of the reeds as I had expected, but on the bank above the watering place, and to my right, the head and part profile of a large leopard came into view. He was watching the antelope, which gave me time for careful aim. I let go the arrow with all the force I could muster.

There followed a great commotion, a blood-curdling growl, as the beast leaped toward me. He seemed to come toward me with the same whiz of speed that my own arrow had taken toward him.

I cannot remember side-stepping that straight yellow streak or reaching for my *fange* sword, or crouching for combat. Yet I must have done all of these things. I do remember that the leopard peeled back his lips, that the bared teeth clicked like gourd shake-shakes, and that its breath was foul. I gathered all my strength behind the plunge of my poisoned *fange* but the brute's claws found me. Blinded by a shower of my own blood streaming down from my scalp, I did not see the paw stroke which knocked the *fange* from my hand. My "one claw" was gone!

Somehow my hands found the animal's throat. The poison on my weapons was taking heavy toll of the beast's strength. I knew I had only to keep my hands pressed on its throat and his claws out of my belly until the poison had finished its work. The animal, even after its eyes began to dim, seemed capable of twisting and turning over inside its fur. My strength was going, too. My legs had been clawed and I slid around in my own blood as I tried to clamp my knees against its ribs. My thumbs gouged into the neck fur where I thought the windpipe should be.

When I felt I could not hold on another moment, I sensed Lamina at my side. Lamina's presence was so real to me that the numbness in my shoulder seemed to be his hand pressing strength into me. Then my senses clouded and I did not feel Lamina's nearness any more.

When I regained consciousness, I was not in the forest. I was in my mother's house. A great many people were doing a great many things. I could not distinguish one person from another. It was like seeing, from a great distance, boulders which might or might not be elephants. Slowly, I sorted them out. The *Alamami* was there crushing tree barks, squeezing berries, bruising leaves. Several lesser medicine men were helping him. The odors of these forest things carried me back to the jungle and my eyes hurt.

I floated through empty space again until the medicine men began pressing my wounds open, making the clawed places gape like mouths to receive the medicines which were being poured into them. I realized dimly through the pain what they were doing. *A leopard kills after he is dead.* This is a bush saying which means that even if a man survives a mauling he is likely to die from infection in the claw wounds.

They bandaged me with leaves and made me drink broths. When they thought I was strong enough to face the sight, they let me look at the calf of my leg. The medicine man told me I would walk again but I did not see how it would be possible. Too much of me was missing. Yet before the moon had filled twice, I was able to hobble over to Lamina's house and sit in the sun with him.

I felt an awkward shyness about speech with Lamina. I knew that I was supposed to speak with him as a fellow hunter, a brother. All of my training had been to regard him as a reverenced master. A certain pride, not to be confused with arrogance, was supposed to be in me now. This was too new to sit on me easily. I was quite sure that it was Lamina who had carried me out of the forest, yet no one would tell me that it was. I wanted to find out but I did not know the proper way to ask. I started by feeling around the edges of the subject. Had Lamina camped at the place where he gave me good-by?

He told me then how he had gone to bed early as was his custom but had not been able to sleep. His heart had beat like a message drum. He had sat up in bed wondering what to do. He had heard the bird of evil omen cry three times, long and wailing. He had risen and collected his weapons. Only then did the bird cease lamenting.

When Lamina was mounted on his horse and headed in the direction of the forest, he said that it seemed to him that the beat of his heart was with that of the earth, so he knew he was doing the right thing.

It was dawn by the time Lamina had found me and bound my wounds with herbs and leaves. He had managed to get me across the horse's back and bring me home, no easy matter since the leopard's blood smell was on me. Afterward, he had gone back to skin the dead leopard.

I was worried about whether I would ever walk right again. A lame man is of little use to his tribe. Lamina was sure that I would. He was right. I have no limp but I bear the scars of the leopard's claws on my left leg.

Song of an Unlucky Man

CHAFF IS in my eye,
A crocodile has me by the leg,
A goat is in the garden,
A porcupine is cooking in the pot,
Meal is drying on the pounding rock,
The King has summoned me to court,
And I must go to the funeral of my mother-in-law:
In short, I am busy.

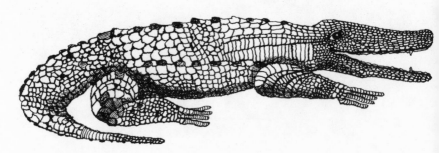

My Wish

BY PHILOMENA KESSEWA KAKA

I WISH I were an eagle
With a piercing golden eye,
For if I were an eagle
I would fly through the sky.

I wish I were a policewoman
In a uniform of blue,
For if I were a policewoman
I would have a whistle too.

I wish I were an Hausaman
With fine things on a tray,
For if I were an Hausaman
I would travel far away.

I wish I were a queen
And had a golden stool,
For if I were a queen
I wouldn't go to school.

45

Lullaby

SOMEONE would like to have you for her child
but you are mine.
Someone would like to rear you on a costly mat
but you are mine.
Someone would like to place you on a camel blanket
but you are mine.
I have you to rear on a torn old mat.
Someone would like to have you as her child
but you are mine.

The Caribbean

Introduction

THE ARC of islands swinging southeastward from Florida to Guyana make up the area called the West Indies. These islands separate the Caribbean Sea from the Atlantic Ocean. The islands resulted from the action of volcanoes, as sunken peaks slowly grew up. In Jamaica some of the mountains rise to 7,000 feet above sea level. The lush greenery of the Caribbean islands has changed little since a poet described the setting as:

> . . . this eternal spring
> Which here enamels everything.

Arawak Indians and Caribs from South America once dwelt on some of the islands, but they were nearly all destroyed by invaders attracted by the tropical areas. Most of the West Indies have been controlled at one time or another by the Spanish, Dutch, French, Americans, or English.

Because of their nearly perfect climate, these islands are excellent places to grow tropical foods: bananas, breadfruit, cocoa, coffee, coconuts, oranges, and sugar cane. The all-important crop sugar cane was introduced into Barbados Island almost 350 years ago. Then for over two centuries European plantation owners transported hundreds of thousands of black men, women, and children from Africa as slaves to work in the West Indian cane fields. This cruel practice of importing slaves was still going on as late as 1863 when the Dutch were the last to stop it. By now of course the larger West Indian islands have gained their independence from the colonial powers.

There are Englishmen, Chinese, Syrians, East Indians, and other nationalities still living in the West Indies. However, so many slaves were brought to the Caribbean that today about eighty percent of all West Indians have some African blood. Therefore, the West Indies are tiny island nations of people who are for the most part of African ancestry.

Africans in the new-world soon forgot their own languages because they were made to speak the European languages of the plantation owners; however, much of the music and folk literature of their African homelands was preserved.

You will find an Anansi spider story in the African section of this book. If you travel throughout the new world you will find Anansi everywhere. In Jamaica he is sometimes called Annancy; in Curacao, Nansi; in South Carolina you might hear some Miss Nancy stories.

In "Anansi and Turtle and Pigeon" Anansi is seen, as usual, near the scene of trouble. Anansi is most popular in Jamaica in the West Indies, though as you can see he doesn't always appear anymore as a spider in stories. In fact, many Jamaicans call *all* folk tales Anansi stories.

The account of the runaway slave, Esteban Montejo, is a true story of his life in the forests of central Cuba. He refused to come out of the forests until after slavery had ended. He was a most inventive man while he kept moving in order to escape capture. What is further remarkable about Mr. Montejo is that in 1963 when he recorded this story of his early life he was 104 years old!

Just as we have read in previous stories how the Milky Way came to be, we can read in "Makonaima Returns" how the country Guyana was founded. This legend tells of how two dark-skinned twin brothers named the land Guyana.

Everywhere people are full of wonder about the beauties of nature. It is understandable that in islands that are mostly rural and agricultural, people would be fascinated by the beauties and mysteries of nature, not only in the daily life of the islands, but also in the sea around them.

Look, for instance, at "The Barracuda," an exciting description of a fishing party which sets off before dawn. The fishermen make some good catches in the waters off Jamaica.

George Lamming tells another story of the sea in "Boy Blue the Crab-Catcher" which is from his autobiography. In his book, he talks of his childhood among friends on Barbados, and how he later went to the larger island of Trinidad.

Whether they are writing about the history of slavery or of the beauty of nature, most of the island writers of the West Indies have taken something of their past from both Africa and Europe and created a distinct kind of writing that is their own.

Living in the Forest

BY ESTABAN MONTEJO

I LED A half-wild existence as a runaway, but the truth is that I lacked for nothing in the forest.

I had to forage for food for a long time, but there was always enough. "The careful tortoise carries his house on his back." I liked vegetables and beans and pork best. I think it is because of the pork that I have lived so long. I used to eat it every day, and it never disagreed with me. I would creep up to the smallholdings at night to catch piglets, taking care that no one heard me. I grabbed the first one I saw by the neck, clapped a halter round it, slung it over my shoulder and started to run, keeping my hand over its snout to stop it squealing. When I reached my camp I set it down and looked it over. If it was well fed and weighed twenty pounds or so, I had meals for a fortnight.

All the forest leaves have their uses. The leaves of tobacco plants and mulberry-trees cure stings. If I saw some insect bite was festering, I picked a tobacco leaf and chewed it thoroughly, then I laid it on the sting and the swelling went. Often, when it was cold, my bones would ache, a dry pain which would not go away. Then I made myself an infusion of rosemary leaves to soothe it, and it was cured at once.

The macaw-tree leaf provided me with smokes. I made

tight-rolled neat little ciagrettes with it. Tobacco was one of
my relaxations. After I left the forest I stopped smoking tobacco, but while I was a runaway I smoked all the time.

And I drank coffee which I made with roast *guanina*
leaves. I had to grind the leaves with the bottom of a bottle.
When the mixture was ground right down, I filtered it and
there was my coffee. I could always add a little wild honey to
give it flavour. Coffee with honey strengthens the organism.
You were always fit and strong in the forest.

Bees' honey is one of the best things there is for health. It
was easy to get in the forest. I used to find it in the hollows of
hardwood trees. I used it to make *chanchanchara,* a delicious
drink made of stream-water and honey, and best drunk cold.
It was better for you than any modern medicine; it was natu-
ral. When there was no stream nearby I hunted around till I
found a spring. In the forest there are springs of sweet water
—the coldest and clearest I have seen in my life—which run
downhill.

I was never short of fire. During my first few days in the forest I had matches. Then they ran out, and I had to use my
yesca, a black ash that I kept in one of the tinderboxes the
Spaniards sold in taverns. It was easy to get a fire going. All
you had to do was rub a stone on the tinderbox till it
sparked.

As I have always liked being my own man, I kept well
away from everyone. I even kept away from the insects. To
frighten off snakes I fired a big log and left it burning all

night. They did not come near because they thought the log
was a devil or an enemy of theirs. That's why I say I enjoyed
my life as a runaway. I looked after myself, and I protected
myself too. I used knives and half-sized machetes made by the
firm of Collins, which were the ones used by the rural police,
to clear the undergrowth and hunt animals, and I kept them
ready in case a *ranchador* tried to take me by surprise—
though that would have been difficult, as I kept on the move.

I spent most of the time walking or sleeping. At midday

and at five in the afternoon I could hear the conch which the women blew to call their husbands home. It sounded like this: "Fuuuu, fu, fu, fu, fu." At night I slept at my ease. That was why I got so fat. I never thought about anything. My life was all eating, sleeping and keeping watch. I liked going to the hills at night; they were quieter and safer. *Ranchadores* and wild animals found difficulty in getting there.

One thing I remember really clearly is the forest birds. They are something I cannot forget. I remember them all. Some were pretty and some were hellishly ugly. They frightened me a lot at first, but then I got used to hearing them. I even got so I felt they were taking care of me. The *cotunto* was a black, *black* bird, which said, "You, you, you, you, you, you, you ate the cheese up." And it kept on saying this till I answered, "Get away!" and it went. I heard it crystal clear. There was another bird which used to answer it as well; it went, "Cu, cu, cu, cu, cu, cu," and sounded like a ghost.

The *sijú* was one of the birds which tormented me most. It always came at night. That creature was the ugliest thing in the forest! It had white feet and yellow eyes. It shrieked out something like this: "Cus, cus, cuuuus."

The barn-owl had a sad song, but then it was a witch. It looked for dead mice. It cried, "Chua, chua, chua, kui, kui," and flew off like a ray of light. When I saw a barn-owl in my path, especially when it was flying to and fro, I used to take a different way because I knew it was warning me of an enemy nearby, or death itself. The barn-owl is wise and strange. I recollect that the witches had a great respect for her and worked magic with her, the *sunsundamba,* as she is called in Africa.

The sparrow came here from Spain and has founded an immense tribe here. Also the *tocororo*, which is half a greenish colour. It wears a scarlet sash across its breast, just like one the King of Spain has. The overseers used to say that it

was a messenger from the King. I know it was forbidden
even to look at a *tocororo*. The Negro who killed one was
killing the King. I saw lots of men get the lash for killing
sparrows and *tocororo*. I liked the *tocororo* because it sang as
if it was hopping about, like this: "Có, co, có, co, có, co."

I got used to living with trees in the forest. They have
their noises too, because the leaves hiss in the air. There is
one tree with a big white leaf which looks like a bird at
night. I could swear that tree spoke. It went, "Uch, uch, uch,
ui, ui, ui, uch, uch." Trees also cast shadows which do no
harm, although one should not walk on them at night. I
think trees' shadows must be like men's spirits.

I stayed on my own as a runaway. I did nothing except listen to the birds and trees, and eat, and I never spoke to a
soul. But when slavery ended I stopped being a runaway. I
realised from the way the people were cheering and shouting
that slavery had ended, and so I came out of the forest. They
were shouting, "We're free now." But I didn't join in, I

thought it might be a lie. I don't know . . . anyway, I went up to a plantation and let my head appear little by little till I was out in the open.

I met an old woman carrying two children in her arms. I called to her, and when she came up I asked her, "Tell me, is it true we are no longer slaves?" She replied, "No, son, we are free now."

The Barracuda

BY ANDREW SALKEY

Seven o'clock: The launch was still at rest on the gently lapping water, for Rory had not yet given the order to move on.

Linda Marsh leant over the side and brushed some bread crumbs off her plate. The water was pale green. The crumbs bobbed up and down on the surface, and, as they became soaked, they began to drift slowly down into the glassy greenness of the lapping half-waves. Linda Marsh watched them for a time, and then she looked away and admired the placid seascape surrounding the launch. She had not experienced such calm and contentment of mind for a long time. She was so caught up in the mood of the setting that she did not see the outline of a huge shape shimmering below the surface of the water.

"What've you been looking at for so long?" Duddy asked her mother.

"Peace and quiet, Duddy," Linda Marsh said. "Something you and your brothers usually don't believe in."

They smiled at each other, and Chod and Zhoosh, who had overheard the remark, pretended to ignore it.

Their mother turned back to look at the water near the side of the launch and gazed down at the massive outline. At first it meant nothing to her. Then slowly she recognised the difference of the colour between the outline and the rest of the water. She stared at it. Still she wasn't sure what to make of it. Then the outline moved slightly, and its mass became immediately more impressive. When that happened a feeling of fear and exhilaration gripped Linda Marsh, and she felt her throat getting dry. At last she found her voice:

"Rory, can you come over here a second?"

He came over, and pointing to the mass in the water she backed away. He looked down, nodded and turned to Quaco,

"Harpoon ready?"

Quaco stiffened like a soldier and then leapt noiselessly into the cabin and in a few seconds emerged with a ten-foot harpoon.

The others on the deck had been duly alerted by Rory. Everybody stood stock still.

Quaco crept quickly up to the side and looked down.

"A wahoo," he said tensely to Rory. Rory nodded.

Linda Marsh hugged herself and moved farther away from the side. Chod and Zhoosh edged towards it. Their father

tried to stop them, but even he felt himself being pulled to the side. Cuffee too was drawing closer to the group.

The seconds went by. Quaco waited for the right moment to strike.

Gathered round him now were Chod, Zhoosh, their father, Cuffee and Rory. Standing well away were Duddy and her mother.

"When?" Quaco asked Rory.

"Any time you're ready," Rory said.

"Got a line 'andy?" asked Quaco.

"There's one fixed in the cabin," Cuffee said.

Quaco raised the harpoon, leant over the side and took his aim deliberately without once glancing at the tip. He kept his arm up and waited to assess the pressure which would be necessary for the thrust of the downward plunge.

"Right!" Rory whispered hoarsely.

But Quaco didn't reply. He was still poised and waiting.

Suddenly Cuffee stepped forward and held Quaco's raised arm. "Give 'im a chance to wrestle wit' you, man," he said compassionately.

Quaco frowned and looked at Rory, who in turn glanced over at Cuffee. In reply, Cuffee smiled wisely.

"O.K. then," Rory said with a shrug.

Quaco lowered his arm and dangled the harpoon aimlessly, while the triangular tip brushed the deck and scraped it in a series of long shallow white lines.

The large mass of the wahoo was still visible in the water near the launch.

Nobody spoke and nobody moved.

Quaco was the first to do so; he muttered, "Cuffee on you' side, wahoo." Then he said enthusiastically, "Awright, so we wrestle 'im then." And he went into the cabin and brought out one of the prepared rods.

"You' usin' the dacron?" Cuffee asked.

Quaco patted the sleek equipment and smiled with uncon-
cealed self-satisfaction.

Cuffee smiled too. And Quaco nodded and said, "Anytime
you ready."

Cuffee looked over the side and breathed in a deep
draught of warm salt air. He held his breath. Then he let it
out and shouted down to the wahoo, and the mass came alive
and vanished.

Rory went into action. He clapped his hands vigorously a
few times. "Right! We're going after him and we'll do it
Cuffee's way," he said. Turning to Cuffee, he ordered, "The
engine! Let her rip!" And to Quaco again, "Sink the bait,
man. Quick!"

The launch throbbed and Cuffee swung it easily into a
left-hand arc and followed what he imagined to be the path
along which the wahoo must have travelled.

Quaco had positioned himself and was holding his breath
with tingling urgency. Chod and Zhoosh were standing behind him and bracing themselves, partly in sympathy and
partly in imitation of his posture.

Cuffee then took the launch on tactically for another three
or four hundred yards in a very wide right-hand arc reducing
the speed at the end of it. Rory signalled and Cuffee cut the
engine.

Seven thirty-five: Nothing. The wahoo had eluded the
launch. Quaco was still standing at his position. Rory was
scanning the water methodically. Cuffee was standing beside
him. Felix Marsh was looking out and hunching his shoulders. Chod and Zhoosh were on either side of him. Duddy
and her mother were sitting on the crossbench behind the
cabin.

There had been very little conversation among them. Yet,
they were all wondering about Cuffee's decision to hunt the

wahoo rather than letting Quaco harpoon it. Chod and
Zhoosh were happy about the sporting chance given to the
fish but they were anxious that Quaco should make a catch as
soon as possible. Cuffee and Rory didn't mind; they were all
for the hunt. So was Quaco. Linda Marsh, however, wasn't
quite sure about the release of the wahoo; she plainly
thought that it was a waste of fishing time and opportunity.
Felix Marsh was open-minded about the matter; he, nev-
ertheless, wanted Quaco to hook something, anything, very
quickly. He believed it would be good for the morale of the
hunt.

Eight o'clock: "Trail it, Quaco!" Rory shouted from the
cabin, as he took over the wheel from Cuffee. He started the
engine and sent the launch tearing through the water.

Quaco trailed the line, after letting it out substantially.

Rory had waited around long enough and he was now
going to try another section of the sea.

The sudden spurt put a new gusto into the party. Everybody approved.

Rory stopped after travelling about a mile.

"Anything?" he called out to Quaco.

Quaco shook his head.

Rory handed over the wheel to Cuffee and got himself a
dacron line and stepped on to the deck.

"You stay where you are, Quaco," he said confidently, "and I'll take the other side."

He fixed his equipment quickly and flicked the line out to the sea.

Chod and Zhoosh separated. Chod went over to his uncle and Zhoosh remained with Quaco.

Eight fifteen: Quaco felt a slight tug at his line; he looked sharply round at Zhoosh and winked.

"Something?" Zhoosh whispered.

"Could be," Quaco whispered back.

"Something big?" asked Zhoosh.

"Not too big, but big enough, I t'ink."

"Still there?"

"Yes, but don't say anyt'ing yet."

Quaco's face became tense. Zhoosh changed his position and stood beside Quaco and looked from the arc of the line back to his face and waited.

But Cuffee had noticed that there was something going on. He knew that Quaco was "feelin' a bite". It was written all over Quaco's face; it was clearly noticeable in the way that his arm muscles were becoming corded, with his back slowly arching, and his feet flatly positioned.

Cuffee shuffled over from the wheel and said,

"You' feelin' a bite, Quaco?"

Quaco nodded.

"Wahoo or wha'?"

"Don't t'ink so, Cuffee."

"Somet'ing smaller?"

"Yes."

"Stay wit' it."

"Sure."

Cuffee went back to the wheel.

Zhoosh continued to ping-pong his eyes between Quaco's face and the line.

Two silver gulls swooped overhead and darted away again.

Cuffee saw the gulls and was confirmed in his suspicion; he was absolutely certain now that Quaco's line was, indeed, "makin' contac'."

Rory's back was turned; he hadn't noticed anything. Neither had Chod nor Duddy, nor their parents.

Quaco was watchful and sensitive. His whole body was tense for action.

Then the second tugging sensation came pulsing along the length of the line and registered its impact in the tendons of Quaco's wrists and forearms. His shoulders twitched. He was assured. It was all up to him. The timing had to be just right, to a split second in fact.

He breathed in, held his breath hard and then jerked the line towards him. The counter-jerk came back at him along the line. He jerked again and it came back a second time. He spun the reel and gave the catch several extra lengths of line.

The others knew that Quaco had held something. They started to encourage him. Rory did not leave his position; he merely turned and shouted, "Big one, Quaco?"

"No," Quaco shouted back. "Feel like a twelve- or fifteen-pound bite."

"*Barracuda?*"

"Maybe, Missa Rory."

Quaco's "maybe" simply meant that it *was* a barracuda. And it was.

It leapt out of the water, about sixty feet away from the launch and began struggling defiantly.

Quaco held on firmly, giving only a certain amount of slack now and then.

By eight twenty-five the one-sided fight was over. The barracuda weighed exactly fifteen pounds.

Boy Blue the Crab-Catcher

BY GEORGE LAMMING

"Let's go," Trumper said. He had hardly spoken when the little crabs appeared. They were nearer the sea now. When we had seen them last they had crawled up to the grape vine, but they must have cut a way back through the sand while we were watching the fisherman. The eyes were raised, and they limped slowly towards the sea. The sand seemed firmer where they were.

"You like crab?" Boy Blue asked. He smiled as he asked the question.

"I like crab," Trumper said, "but these too small." He too smiled as he spoke.

"What don't kill does fatten," Boy Blue said.

Boy Blue left us and crept towards the crabs approaching them from the back. Crab-catching was a pastime which we used to test our speed as well as lightness of touch. After heavy rains the village was often invaded by crabs, large blue-back creatures sprawling stupidly here and there to get their bearings. The men and boys came out in droves with sticks and pokers and traps of every description. Children and women screamed when they saw the catch. Sometimes it yielded hundreds of crabs, and the boys and men who had trapped them made a prosperous business. Even those who had condemned crab-catching as a dirty sport bought them. They were delicious if you prepared them well. But these crabs that leaned uncertainly on the slope of the shore were different. They were very small and decorous, like cups and saucers which my mother bought and put away. You couldn't use them for drinking purposes. They were too delicate and decorous. These little crabs had that quality. Small, enchanting bits of furniture with which the shore was decorated. You wouldn't eat them although the meat might have been as delicious as that of the big village crabs, which were ugly and gross in their crawling movements.

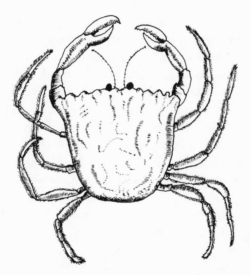

Boy Blue didn't really want to eat one of these. He wanted to catch them as a kind of triumph. He could show what he had done after spending so many hours on the other side of the lighthouse. Catching things gave us little boys a great thrill. Sometimes we shot birds and carried them exposed in the palm of the hand. Everyone could see what we had done, meaning what he had achieved. It was like talking to the

fisherman, or climbing a mountain which no one had hith-
erto dared ascend. The thrill of capturing something! It was
wonderful! Boy Blue looked like a big crab crawling on all
fours, and he made us laugh with the shift and shake of his
slouching movements. The crabs dropped their eyes and remained still. It was always very difficult to tell what a crab
would do. Sometimes they would scamper wildly if you were
a mile away, and at other times they would crouch and bun-
dle themselves together the nearer you approached. They
seemed to feel that they were unseen because their eyes were
dropped level in the slot that contained them. Boy Blue lay
flat on the sand with his hands stretched out full length. The
crabs were trying to make a way in the sand. They had seen
him but there was no great hurry in escaping. Perhaps the
sand was their domain. They could appear and disappear at
will while you waited and watched. His hands had them covered but there was no contact. The difficulties had only
started. When you were catching a crab with bare hands you
required great skill. You had to place your thumb and index
finger somewhere between the body and the claws of the
crab. That was very tricky, since the crabs' claws were free
like revolving chairs. They could spin, it seemed, in all direc-
tions, and they raised and dropped them to make any angle.
Hundreds of boys were squeezed time and again in their
effort to trap the carbs barehanded. If you missed the grip, or
gripped a minute too soon the claws had clinched you. And
the claws cut like blades. You had to know your job. You had
to be a crab catcher, as we would say.

A master at the art, Boy Blue considered he was. He had
caught several in his time. The art had become a practised
routine. It was simply a matter of catching them. In this art
he carried the same assurance and command we had noticed
in the fisherman. He lay flat with his hands pressed on the
crabs' backs. He was trying to gather them up all together.

His thumb had found the accustomed spot between the claw and the body of the crab. The crabs were still but buckled tight, so that it was difficult to strengthen the grip. Sometimes they seemed to understand the game. They remained still and stiffly buckled, and when you least expected the claws flashed like edged weapons.

The waves came up and the sand slid back. It seemed they would escape. If the waves came up again the sand would be loosened and they could force a way easily into the sand. Boy Blue had missed his grip. The wave came again and the sand sloped. Boy Blue slid back and the crabs were free from his grip. He propelled his feet in the sand in an attempt to heave himself forward. His weight pressed down. The wave receded and the sand shifted sharply. He came to a kneeling position and the sand slipped deeper. The crabs were safe. He threw his hand up and stood. The sand shifted under his feet and the waves hastening to the shore lashed him face downward. The salt stung his eyes and he groped to his feet. Another wave heaved and he tottered. The crabs! The crabs had disappeared. We could not understand what was happening. Boy Blue was laughing. It made us frighten the way he laughed. A wave wrenched him and now he was actually in the sea. We shivered, dumb. A wave pushed him up, and another completing the somersault plunged him down. He screamed and we screamed too. He was out of sight and we screamed with all the strength of our lungs. And the waves washed our screams up the shore. It was like a conspiracy of waves against the crab catcher. We screamed and the fisherman came out from behind the lighthouse. We motioned him to the spot where we had last seen Boy Blue. There was a faint scream in the air. We could not understand how it had happened. We could not follow the speed of the fisherman's movements. He had gathered up the net and tossed it in the sea over the area we had indicated. He hauled ear-

nestly and the body of the net emerged with the strangest of
all catches. Boy Blue was there. He was rolled up like a wet
blanket. We were dumb with fright. He looked so impotent
in the net. His eyes were bloodshot and his body heaved with
a great flood of wind. He gasped and gasped, like a dog that
had strained itself with too great speed in the chase. The
fisherman hauled him up the beach and emptied the net as if
it contained a useless dead thing. He looked at Boy Blue
with a kind of disgust. Boy Blue was like a fly which had
buzzed too long. You slapped it down and were sorry that
you made such a mess of your hands. You might have left it.
But you couldn't. It was unbearable. A necessary evil. Slap-

ping it down. That's what it was. A necessary evil. The
fisherman looked down at Boy Blue, unspeaking. There was
no trace of what we would call bad temper. Just a kind of
quiet disgust. Boy Blue sat silent, his teeth chattering and his
whole body a shiver of flesh in the wind. We could not speak.
We were afraid of the fisherman. The way he looked at us!
He was like someone who had been sorry for what he did,
and yet not sorry since he knew it had to be done. He looked
so terribly repentant and at the same time there was an ex-
pression which we could not define. Under the marble eyes
and the impenetrable stare there must have been something
that cried out for life. He knew the catch was not a fish, but

he hauled the net with the earnestness that could only have meant a desire beyond his control for the other's survival. Now he looked so terribly penitent. We were frightened.

"I should have let you drown," he snarled, and his voice held terror.

"Thank you, sir," Boy Blue said, catching his breath. It was the first time Boy Blue had spoken.

"By Christ, you should have drown," the fisherman snarled again.

"You mustn't say that," Boy Blue said. We were stunned by the impertinence of the words. But there couldn't have been impertinence. Boy Blue was shivering like a kitten that had had a bath.

"Why the heck shouldn't I have let you drown?" the fisherman shouted. It was the first thing he had said that made us think he was really human like us. The way he said it! He now looked angry.

"Tell me," he snapped. "Tell me to my face why I shouldn't have let you drown?"

" 'Cause if I'd drown I wouldn't have been able to tell you thanks," Boy Blue said. He was serious and the fisherman walked back towards the lighthouse.

Anansi and Turtle and Pigeon

Turtle once lived next door to Pigeon, and across the road was Anansi's house. Sometimes Turtle and Anansi would stand together and watch Pigeon flying from one house-top to another, from one tree to another.

"I wish I could fly with Pigeon," said Turtle.

"I wish so, too," said Anansi.

At last one day they went to Pigeon and asked him to teach them to fly. Pigeon took them to the oldest pigeon of all. He looked as wise as an owl and said that they could learn. Then each pigeon pulled out a feather and glued it to Turtle's back until he looked like a pincushion, all full of feathers. Anansi, they said, would have to let Turtle try first. Next they took hold of Turtle and flew up into the air.

Soon they reached Tiger's cornfield. Every day the pigeons went there and took Tiger's corn. When they got there they took their feathers away from Turtle, gave him a large bag, and told him to pick up the grains of corn from the ground. So they all picked up corn; and Turtle picked up corn, too.

Then they heard a noise.

The pigeons all stood still and lifted up their heads. A second or two later the oldest pigeon flapped his wings and rose up, and all the other pigeons flapped their wings and flew away, leaving Turtle all by himself in the field of corn. Anansi saw the pigeons return home, but there was no Turtle with them. Turtle was left in the middle of the field, and there the watchman found him with the bag of corn.

"So it's you, Turtle, is it? You are the thief that comes and steals Tiger's corn?"

"No," cried Turtle, "no, my sweet watchman. Ask Anansi if you doubt me. It is the pigeons that come stealing the corn."

"What are you doing here, then?" asked the watchman.

"Oh, my sweet watchman," cried Turtle, "ask Anansi if you doubt me. I told the pigeons that I wanted to fly, and they lent me feathers and I came with them; but I am not stealing the corn."

"Well," said the watchman, "I never yet saw a turtle fly. You must come with me." And he put Turtle in a pail of water and took him to Tiger's house.

Now Turtle remembered what Anansi had once told him. Anansi once said: "Turtle, when you don't know what to say and when you don't know what to do—sing!" So Turtle began to sing. He sang so sweetly that the watchman began to dance, and he danced until he had spilled all the water out

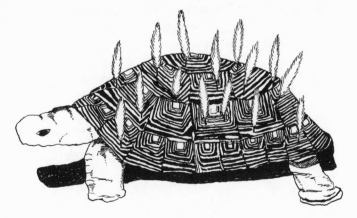

of the pail. Then Turtle called out, "If you let me walk I will sing so sweetly!"

But the watchman said no.

At last they came to Tiger's house, and Tiger came out to see Turtle.

"Ah," said Tiger, "call the cook!" Tiger told the cook how to stew Turtle for supper, and then he went off to invite his relations and friends to come to the meal.

Now the cook was mixing all the onions and pimento together, and Turtle remembered what Anansi had said, and Turtle began to sing. He sang so sweetly that the cook began to dance.

Then Turtle said, "My sweet cook, if you will only put me on the ground outside I will sing so sweetly!"

The cook put Turtle outside, and he sang more sweetly than ever; and the cook danced all the time.

Then Turtle said: "Oh, my sweet cook, if you will take me to the river and put just the tip of my tail in the water I will sing more sweetly than ever."

The cook took Turtle to the river and put just the tip of his tail in the water, and Turtle sang more sweetly than ever, and the cook danced and danced.

But soon she heard no singing. She looked down.

There was Turtle at the bottom of the river! And Turtle waved his hand and swam away.

And the cook dared not go back to Tiger's house.

That is why, from that day to this, no one cooks Tiger's food for him.

Makonaima Returns

BY HENRY W. JOSIAH

THERE was a time when the earth was young. The trees in the forests were little. The hills were still growing up to be mountains. The rivers running down to the sea were small streams rushing round hillsides like children playing. The rocks were not yet hard and old but were soft and gentle like the face of a baby.

And in those far-off times our people, the Cariama, lived near the Great Spirit in the Place of the Sun above the skies. Listen to the birds singing at Sunrise and you will hear how the Cariama came down from the Place to live in Guyana.

Makonaima was fifteen earth years old. He and his twin brother, Pia used to wander about in the endless vastness of the Place of the Sun above the skies, seeking to learn more and more about everything. They had already learned their school lessons well. They knew many things and they understood much, as you will one day understand.

They could tell you about numbers bigger than the biggest number you ever heard about. They could tell you about things smaller than the smallest thing anyone could ever see or touch. They could tell you where the Great Spirit came from who had made all things and all men. And they could tell you, if you asked, who had made the Maker of all men. They knew so much, but they wanted to know much more. For this is the way of great men.

The brothers Makonaima and Pia were dark-skinned and their eyes twinkled between and behind the long slanting narrowness of their eyelids. The people of the Place of the Sun had squinting eyes because of the eternal brightness of the Place. Their skins were dark because of the sun in whose warmth they lived always.

One day Makonaima looked down through a hole in the skies and he saw the earth below with hills and forests and savannahs and rivers running down to the gentle waters of the wide, wide seas.

He was not surprised, for wise people are not surprised when they discover new things. They know the Great Spirit made all things and made them well.

Makonaima was pleased. He called out to his brother.

Pia came and looked down through the hole in the skies.

"Let us go down and learn more about this place which is so beautiful," he said.

Makonaima hesitated, thinking of the best way to make the journey down. He and his brother were both eager to start this new journey.

They let down a rope ladder through the hole in the skies and they climbed down. They came down on the top of a young mountain which was so beautiful that Pia said it reminded him of their mother's breasts from which they both used to feed as babies.

"Let's name it after our mother," he suggested. Makonaima agreed. "Yes," he said, "we will call it Roraima, for that is our mother's name."

"And those other little mountains," Pia exclaimed, "They are like our little sisters. Yes?"

"Indeed," Makonaima agreed, "so we will name them after our sisters, the Pakaraimas."

The twin brothers wandered about the earth, picking and eating delicious fruits and nuts and delighting in the fragrance of the lovely flowers and the clear melodic calls of the many-coloured birds and the butterflies that flew from tree to tree and from flower to flower.

They built a raft and floated down the rivers until they reached the sea. "This place," Pia observed shrewdly, "is a land of many waters. The rivers run and run and never seem to stop. They go on and on like that aunt of ours who, when she comes to visit, never seems to stop talking—the one we love best of all because of her lovely stories. You know who I mean."

"Guyana," said Makonaima.

"The same one," said Pia. "We love this place as we love her, don't we?"

"Well then," Makonaima decided quickly, "this place is Guyana."

But there was one strange thing about this new place that the twin brothers had to get themselves accustomed to quickly. That was the quickness with which day changed into night, and night into day again. You see, in the Place of the Sun a day lasts a long, long time, longer than on earth. And this was why, although the twin brothers came down to spend a day on earth, they really had been spending many days.

Too soon it was time to return to their home in the Place of the Sun. But when they travelled back to the top of Roraima where they had left the rope ladder hanging they found the ladder gone. And there was no other way to go back up through the hole in the skies.

Then Makoniama made another discovery on the soft rocks of the mountain side. "Look Pia," he exclaimed, "look at those footprints; they are not ours. Others have been here since we came."

It was true. The footprints went off in a different direction from the one they themselves had taken.

Pia nodded thoughtfully. "You are right," he said. "Others have come down the ladder after us, but they, too, have not gone up again."

After a while they heard voices—familiar voices. Makonaima smiled. "It is Mazaruni and Cuyuni, our classmates."

Pia pretended to groan. "I should have known; those two girls keep following us all over. They're always causing us endless trouble."

"You shouldn't speak like that about them," Makonaima said. "You know Cuyuni loves you more than anyone else in the whole of the Place."

"Aha!" Pia smiled teasingly, "And we both know that you love Mazaruni so much you might have cried a river of tears if you had never been able to see her again."

When the girls arrived and heard that someone had pulled

up the rope ladder, they were not worried. Rather they seemed pleased about it. They said: "We are satisfied to wait here with you even if we wait forever. We will help you gather fruits and nuts to eat."

And so they waited for the ladder to be let down again. They waited for many sun months, which in earth time is many years. And while they waited they grew older, and Makonaima married Mazaruni, and Pia married Cuyuni. And later they had many children and grandchildren who went wandering about Guyana, setting up villages and cultivating the land and reaping crops and fishing and hunting as our people do to this day.

The four who had arrived from the Place of the Sun grew very old. Pia died and was buried on the spot where they had landed on Roraima. Cuyuni and Mazaruni went away with their grandchildren to villages far from Roraima.

But Makoniama remained on the mountain he and his brother had named after their mother. He was certain, he said, that if he stayed there he would be able one day to climb up the ladder again through the hole in the skies and return home to the Place of the Sun.

The young ones came often to visit and bring food and cassiri for the old man to eat and drink. And they used to say, "Yes. O Makoniama. It is as you say, Makoniama."

They said this out of respect for him, but really they did not believe that such a thing would be. They came to visit and left him with his food and drink, and the company of the birds who sang for him all day from sunrise to sunset.

And then one day, when they came again to visit, Makonaima was not there. The best trackers searched diligently but they found not a trace of him. Nor could they find any trace of Pia's grave. And they discovered another strange thing: the birds were singing on the mountain top no more.

Makoniama has returned to the Place of the Sun, they said.

The next morning, at daybreak, they stood on Mount Roraima, these children of Makonaima, watching the rising sun, reverently. No birds sang.

And Rima, who was one of the youngest of Makoniama's many grandchildren, clasped her arms across her breast and whispered the words she had heard the others say so often—"Yes, O Makoniama. It is as you say, Makoniama."

She said this out of respect for him, but she also believed that it was true—that Makoniama had indeed returned to the Place of the Sun above the skies.

And suddenly the sunlit mountain top burst into a glory of bird song. The singing birds flew up into the air and out over the mountains and the hills and savannahs and down the long brown rivers to the sea, telling and re-telling the story of Makoniama. Listen to them when the sun is rising, and you will hear the story too.

Madam Crab Loses Her Head

T HERE was once, in the forest of South Trinidad, an extremely old woman named En-Bois-Chinan. No one, except Madam Crab, knew anything about her, not even her name, and Madam Crab was so old and crotchety that no one ever bothered to ask her questions. En-Bois-Chinan was an ugly old woman, with skin a dark brown like the colour of roasted coffee beans, and deep dark wrinkles on her face and hands. She had short thick hair, as grey as ashes, and her small eyes, sunken into her face, were almost hidden by bushy, grey-black eyebrows.

On the edge of that same forest, there lived a wood-cutter, his wife, and their little daughter, Ula. The little girl was 8 years old. She was black skinned, with very short, black hair, and her deep brown eyes were bright and lively. When she laughed her small white teeth sparkled and dimples appeared in her cheeks.

Ula loved to collect wild flowers. One day, when she had collected a great many of them, and played hide and seek with her shadow between the trees, she grew very tired, and lay down to rest. When she awoke, the sun had disappeared and the forest had grown dark. She was frightened. The daytime sounds of birds whistling, and leaves rustling in a gentle

breeze had changed to the croaking of frogs and the humming of night insects. In her hurry to get home, she chose
the wrong path and without knowing it, went deeper and
deeper into the forest. It became darker and lonelier. She
hurried on, looking to left and right for some sign that she
was nearing home, but none appeared. She was lost.

Suddenly, she heard a coarse, gruff voice saying, "Who is
there? Who is there?" Too frightened to answer, Ula darted
behind what seemed to be a short, crooked stump, but
turned out to be the old woman—En-Bois-Chinan—herself.
The old woman held her tightly and said, "Who are you?
What is your name? No one comes into this part of the forest! Answer me!"

"My name is Ula," the little girl cried, "and I am lost.
Please show me the way home to my parents. I live on the
edge of the forest." But En-Bois-Chinan said, "No, come with
me. The forest is too dark. Tomorrow I will show you the
way."

Ula was afraid of the old woman, but even more afraid of

the forest, so she went quietly. When they got to the hut, the old woman gave her a piece of hot roasted johnny-bake, and a light tea made from the shining bush plant and sweetened with plenty of cow's milk and sugar. Once Ula had eaten, it was not long before she fell asleep, and En-Bois-Chinan, looking at a little girl for the first time in so many dozens of years, began to think up schemes which would keep her in the forest forever.

When Ula awoke next morning, she was anxious to be off, but the old woman had very different plans. She said:

"Why must you go home? Stay with me. I have no one to keep me company or help me with my work. I don't think that I will let you go at all."

"Oh! What shall I do, what shall I do?" wailed Ula. "Please let me go home," She cried and cried until her eyes were red and swollen, En-Bois-Chinan did everything she could to make her stop crying. She promised her lots of nice things to eat, but Ula cried all the more. En-Bois-Chinan coaxed and scolded in turns, and then at last she said, "Very well, you may go. I will show you the way, but first you must tell me my name."

"Oh, that is easy," Ula said.

"Not as easy as you think," En-Bois-Chinan warned, and the girl started guessing.

"Is it Belle?" said Ula.

"No, it isn't," said the old woman.

"Is it Tina," said Ula.

"No, it isn't," said the old woman.

"Is it Yola, Una, Gloria . . ." asked Ula.

"No, it isn't, no it isn't," said the old woman.

Ula called every name she could remember, still the old woman said, "No it isn't."

"What can your name be," Ula cried. "I know! You don't mean to let me go. You have no name at all." But En-Bois-

Chinan said, "I have a name. Call it, and I will show you the way home." Then she took up her cutlass and went into the forest for the day.

Ula walked all over the hut and garden to see whether the name was written anywhere. She questioned every insect and creature she met. "Mr. Cricket, Mr. Cricket, do you know the old woman's name?"

"Not I, not I," said the Cricket, "no one ever calls her, you see."

"Mr. Grasshopper, Mr. Grasshopper, do you know the old woman's name?"

"Not I, not I," said the Grasshopper, and so it went on all during the day until the old woman came home. When she had put down her basket of herbs and her cutlass, she said to Ula:

"Hello, little girl, do you know my name?"

"Is it Ann, Margaret, Pamela, Stella?" said Ula, calling all the names she had remembered during the day.

"No," said En-Bois-Chinan. "It isn't! And now it is time for your dinner and bed.

Next morning En-Bois-Chinan went again into the forest, and Ula, opening the garden gate, wandered out among the trees and tall grass. "Do you know the old woman's name?" she asked every creature she met. But they all answered, "No, we don't, no one ever calls her, you see."

The day passed and the old woman came back to the hut. Putting down her basket of herbs and her cutlass, she said, "Little girl, do you know my name?"

"Is it Mary, Rhona, Joan?" said Ula, calling more names she had remembered during the day, but the old woman answered, "No, it is not, and now it is time for your supper and bed."

Again next morning, the old woman took her cutlass and basket and went into the forest. Ula wandered out of the garden, through the trees and bushes, down to the river. She was tired of asking questions, and very, very sad. Sure now that she would never discover the old woman's name, and never see her parents again, she sat by the river and cried.

Suddenly, a croaky old voice said, "Who is making that loud noise?"

Madam Crab had come out of her hole, gundies snapping, to drive away her unwelcome visitor. But when she saw Ula crying her heart out, she felt very sorry for her and asked:

"Why are you crying, little girl?"

"Because I can't find out the old woman's name."

"But why do you want to know her name?"

"She will not show me the way home to my parents until I can call her name," Ula answered. "I've asked and asked, but no one knows."

"What a wicked old woman," Madam Crab exclaimed. "But don't you worry. You have come to the right person. I know the old woman's name. I am as old as she is, and I remember her name well."

"Oh, what is it? What is it?" Ula cried joyfully. "Tell me, tell me."

"Her name," said Crab, "is. . . . Let me see now . . . um . . . it's something about wood, but spoken in patois, you know. Oh, I remember! It is En-Bois-Chinan. Yes, En-Bois-Chinan. You see, I told you I would remember."

"En-Bois-Chinan," Ula said. "What an odd name. I would never have guessed it. What does it mean?"

"It's the name of a wood," said the Crab, "a wood with a bitter bark. It suits her, too."

"Oh, thank you, thank you, Crab," said Ula, and lifting up the old crab, she kissed her all over.

"Careful, careful," cried the Crab. "I'm too old for such treatment." But she liked it just the same.

"The old woman will soon be home," Ula said. "I must go."

"Good luck," said the crab, "I hope she keeps her promise."

When the old woman got home, she put down her basket and cutlass, and said, "Well, little girl, what is my name?"

"Your name," answered Ula slowly, "is En-Bois-Chinan. I found out, you see. Now you must let me go."

En-Bois-Chinan was very surprised, but she said, "I will keep my promise. Come, I will show you the way home."

She took Ula by the hand and led her to the track she should follow. "This is the path you must take," she said. "But first, tell me, how did you find out?"

"Someone told me," said Ula. "But I can't tell you who it is."

"Tell me, tell me," said the old woman, drawing closer to her. But Ula moved swiftly. She tugged her hand away from the old woman, and went running down the path as quickly as her legs would carry her.

En-Bois-Chinan went back to the house and picked up her cutlass. Then she went out again, and every creature she met she asked, "Did you tell the little girl my name?"

"Which little girl," a Jack Spaniard answered.

"I don't know your name," a ground worm replied.

But when she came to the river, Madam Crab said proudly, "Yes, you wicked old woman, I told her your name. I am as old as you are, and I'm the only one who knows your name."

The old woman was very angry. She lifted the cutlass and bringing it down very quickly, cut the old crab's head off with one swipe, and this is why a crab has no head up to today.

Madam Crab was stunned, and in pain, but she said, "Cut off my head if you like, you wicked old woman. The little girl is safe, but you are still alone with your temper and your bad manners. You've taken my head, but after all, I still have my back. Crick, crack!"

United States

Introduction

Today, our population of more than two hundred million is well over ten percent Negro, giving America one of the largest black populations of any nation in the world. Negroes are America's largest minority group and, aside from Indians, by far our oldest.

The first black men in America were one hundred slaves brought by the Spanish who founded a town in 1526 in what is now South Carolina. That same year, those slaves rebelled at the cruel treatment they received, killed some of their masters, and fled to the Indians.

Never in any period of American history have Negroes *accepted* a condition of slavery or inferiority. From that first bloody rebellion of 1526 onwards, there were literally hundreds of slave uprisings. However, since slaves were nearly always poorly armed and always outnumbered, these rebellions never had any great success.

Despite their lack of opportunities, black people have been extremely important in building America's strength. They have fought in large numbers in every war beginning with the American Revolution. They have made important contributions in the fields of music, folklore, theater, poli-science, sports, and literature. The list could go on and on.

The Negro writings in this section will give you some understanding of the experiences and feelings of black Americans, not only in the twentieth century, but also back in earlier times when slavery existed. The most important writing on slavery has understandably come from the slaves themselves as in Charles Ball's "recital" of his life. Clearly, the children in slavery were treated no better than the adults— at age four, Charles Ball, who still had "never had on clothes" in his life, was sold away from his mother. The account of Ball's early life is a sorrowful narration of a child being separated from both father and mother, which almost always occurred in slavery.

Some years after the end of the Civil War, Nat Love told of his adventures as a black cowboy out West. The part included here tells how he managed to outwit some Indians.

In a brief poem written in about 1920, Langston Hughes summarizes his feelings about being Negro. In his autobiography, he said that he wrote the poem "I've Known Rivers" in about fifteen minutes on the back of an envelope just after his train crossed the Mississippi. He thinks of all the slaves who were sold down the river, and recalls other rivers which were connected with the Negro past, and how in the long history of the race the Negro's soul has grown deep like rivers.

Langston Hughes' story "Thank You, M'am" was written nearly forty years after this poem and treats a subject which was always important to him—human understanding and sympathy. His feeling for people is shown clearly in "Let America Be America Again," in which he pleads for a better life for the poor white, the red man, the refuge, and the Negro.

As you continue reading American Literature in school, you will discover that some of America's greatest writers in the twentieth century have been Negroes. Like all good writers, they document the human experience. Their works also have a further importance, since they explain how it is to be a black person living in America.

Fifty Years in Chains

BY CHARLES BALL

SEPARATED FROM MY MOTHER

My STORY is a true one, and I shall tell it in a simple style. It will be merely a recital of my life as a slave in the Southern States of the Union—a description of Negro slavery in the "model Republic."

My grandfather was brought from Africa and sold as a slave in Calvert county, in Maryland. I never understood the name of the ship in which he was imported, nor the name of the planter who bought him on his arrival, but at the time I knew him he was a slave in a family called Maud, who resided near Leonardtown.

My father was a slave in a family named Hauty, living near the same place. My mother was the slave of a tobacco planter, who died when I was about four years old. My mother had several children, and they were sold upon master's death to separate purchasers. She was sold, my father told me, to a Georgia trader. I, of all her children, was the only one left in Maryland.

When sold I was naked, never having had on clothes in my life, but my new master gave me a child's frock, belonging to one of his own children. After he had purchased me, he dressed me in this garment, took me before him on his horse, and started home; but my poor mother, when she saw me leaving her for the last time, ran after me, took me down from the horse, clasped me in her arms, and wept loudly and bitterly over me.

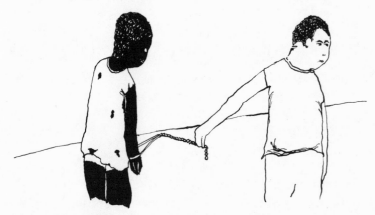

My master seemed to pity her, and endeavored to soothe her distress by telling her that he would be a good master to me, and that I should not want anything. She then, still holding me in her arms, walked along the road beside the horse as he moved slowly, and earnestly and imploringly besought my master to buy her and the rest of her children, and not permit them to be carried away by the Negro buyers. Whilst thus entreating him to save her and her family, the slave-driver, who had first bought her, came running in pursuit of her with a raw-hide in his hand. When he overtook us, he told her he was her master now, and ordered her to give that little Negro to its owner, and come back with him.

My mother then turned to him and cried, "Oh, master, do not take me from my child!" Without making any reply, he gave her two or three heavy blows on the shoulders with his raw-hide, snatched me from her arms, handed me to my master, and seizing her by one arm, dragged her back towards the place of sale. My master then quickened the pace of his horse; and as we advanced, the cries of my poor parent became more and more indistinct—at length they died away in the distance, and I never again heard the voice of my poor mother.

Young as I was, the horrors of that day sank deeply into my heart, and even at this time, though half a century has elapsed, the terrors of the scene return with painful vividness upon my memory. Frightened at the sight of the cruelties inflicted upon my poor mother, I forgot my own sorrows at parting from her and clung to my new master, as an angel and a saviour, when compared with the hardened fiend into whose power she had fallen.

She had been a kind and good mother to me; had warmed me in her bosom in the cold nights of winter; and had often divided the scanty pittance of food allowed her by her mistress, between my brothers, and sisters, and me, and gone supperless to bed herself. Whatever victuals she could obtain beyond the coarse food, salt fish and corn bread, allowed to slaves on the Patuxent and Potomoc rivers, she carefully distributed among her children, and treated us with all the tenderness which her own miserable condition would permit. I have no doubt that she was chained and driven to Carolina, and toiled out the residue of a forlorn and famished existence in the rice swamps, or indigo fields of the South.

My father never recovered from the effects of the shock, which this sudden and overwhelming ruin of his family gave him. He had formerly been of a gay, social temper, and when he came to see us on a Saturday night, he always brought us some little present, such as the means of a poor slave would allow—apples, melons, sweet potatoes, or, if he could procure nothing else, a little parched corn, which tasted better in our cabin, because he had brought it.

He spent the greater part of the time, which his master

permitted him to pass with us, in relating such stories as he had learned from his companions, or in singing the songs common amongst the slaves of Maryland and Virginia. After this time I never heard him laugh heartily, or sing a song. He became gloomy and morose in his temper, to all but me; and spent nearly all his leisure time with my grandfather, who claimed kindred with some royal family in Africa, and had been a great warrior in his native country.

The master of my father was a hard, penurious man, and so exceedingly avaricious, that he scarcely allowed himself the common conveniences of life. A stranger to sensibility, he was incapable of tracing the change in the temper and deportment of my father, to its true cause; but attributed it to a sullen discontent with his condition as a slave, and a desire to abandon his service, and seek his liberty by escaping to some of the free States.

To prevent the perpetration of this suspected crime of *running away from slavery,* the old man resolved to sell my father to a Southern slave-dealer, and accordingly applied to one of those men, who was at that time in Calvert, to become the purchaser. The price was agreed on, but, as my father was a very strong, active, and resolute man, it was deemed unsafe for the Georgian to attempt to seize him, even with the aid of others, in the day-time, when he was at work, as it was known he carried upon his person a large knife.

It was therefore determined to secure him by stratagem, and for this purpose, a farmer in the neighborhood, who was made privy to the plan, alleged that he had lost a pig, which must have been stolen by some one, and that he suspected my father to be the thief. A constable was employed to arrest him, but as he was afraid to undertake the business alone, he called on his way, at the house of the master of my grandfather, to procure assistance from the overseer of the plantation. When he arrived at the house, the overseer was at the barn, and thither he repaired to make his application.

At the end of the barn was the coach-house, and as the day was cool, to avoid the wind which was high, the two walked to the side of the coach-house to talk over the matter, and settle their plan of operations. It so happened that my grandfather, whose business it was to keep the coach in good condition, was at work at this time, rubbing the plated handles of the doors, and brightening the other metallic parts of the vehicle. Hearing the voice of the overseer without, he suspended his work, and listening attentively, became a party to their councils. They agreed that they would delay the execution of their project until the next day, as it was then late. They supposed they would have no difficulty in apprehending their intended victim, as, knowing himself innocent of the theft, he would readily consent to go with the constable to a justice of the peace, to have the charge examined.

That night, however, about midnight, my grandfather silently repaired to the cabin of my father, a distance of about three miles, aroused him from his sleep, made him acquainted with the extent of his danger, gave him a bottle of cider and a small bag of parched corn, and then enjoined him to fly from the destination which awaited him. In the morning the Georgian could not find his newly purchased slave, who was never seen or heard of in Maryland from that day.

Outwitting the Indians

BY NAT LOVE

IT WAS a bright, clear fall day, October 4, 1876, that quite
a large number of us boys started out over the range hunting
strays which had been lost for some time. We had scattered
over the range and I was riding along alone when all at once
I heard the well known Indian war whoop and noticed not
far away a large party of Indians making straight for me.
They were all well mounted and they were in full war paint,
which showed me that they were on the war path, and as I
was alone and had no wish to be scalped by them I decided
to run for it.

So I headed for Yellow Horse Canyon and gave my horse
the rein, but as I had considerable objection to being chased
by a lot of painted savages without some remonstrance, I
turned in my saddle every once in a while and gave them a
shot by way of greeting, and I had the satisfaction of seeing a
painted brave tumble from his horse and go rolling in the
dust every time my rifle spoke, and the Indians were by no
means idle all this time, as their bullets were singing around
me rather lively, one of them passing through my thigh, but
it did not amount to much. Reaching Yellow Horse Canyon,
I had about decided to stop and make a stand when one of
their bullets caught me in the leg, passing clear through it

and then through my horse, killing him. Quickly falling behind him I used his dead body for a breast work and stood
the Indians off for a long time, as my aim was so deadly and
they had lost so many that they were careful to keep out of
range.

But finally my ammunition gave out, and the Indians were
quick to find this out, and they at once closed in on me, but
I was by no means subdued, wounded as I was and almost
out of my head, and I fought with my empty gun until
finally overpowered. When I came to my senses I was in the
Indians' camp.

My wounds had been dressed with some kind of herbs, the
wound in my breast just over the heart was covered thickly
with herbs and bound up. My nose had been nearly cut off,
also one of my fingers had been nearly cut off. These wounds
I received when I was fighting my captors with my empty
gun. What caused them to spare my life I cannot tell, but it
was I think partly because I had proved myself a brave man,
and all savages admire a brave man and when they captured

a man whose fighting powers were out of the ordinary they generally kept him if possible as he was needed in the tribe.

Then again Yellow Dog's tribe was composed largely of half breeds, and there was a large percentage of colored blood in the tribe, and as I was a colored man they wanted to keep me, as they thought I was too good a man to die. Be that as it may, they dressed my wounds and gave me plenty to eat, but the only grub they had was buffalo meat which they cooked over a fire of buffalo chips, but of this I had all I wanted to eat. For the first two days after my capture they kept me tied hand and foot. At the end of that time they untied my feet, but kept my hands tied for a couple of days longer, when I was given my freedom, but was always closely watched by members of the tribe.

Three days after my capture my ears were pierced and I was adopted into the tribe. The operation of piercing my ears was quite painful, in the method used, as they had a small bone secured from a deer's leg, a small thin bone, rounded at the end and as sharp as a needle. This they used to make the holes, then strings made from the tendons of a deer were inserted in place of thread, of which the Indians had none. Then horn ear rings were placed in my ears and the same kind of salve made from herbs which they placed on my wounds was placed on my ears and they soon healed.

The bullet holes in my leg and breast also healed in a surprisingly short time. That was good salve all right. As soon as I was well enough I took part in the Indian dances. One kind or another was in progress all the time. The war dance and the medicine dance seemed the most popular. When in the war dance the savages danced around me in a circle, making gestures, chanting, with every now and then a blood curdling yell, always keeping time to a sort of music provided by stretching buffalo skins tightly over a hoop.

When I was well enough I joined the dances, and I think I

soon made a good dancer. The medicine dance varies from the war dance only that in the medicine dance the Indians danced around a boiling pot, the pot being filled with roots and water and they dance around it while it boils. The medicine dance occurs about daylight.

I very soon learned their ways and to understand them, though our conversation was mostly carried on by means of signs. They soon gave me to understand that I was to marry the chief's daughter, promising me 100 ponies to do so, and she was literally thrown in my arms; as for the lady she seemed perfectly willing if not anxious to become my bride. She was a beautiful woman, or rather girl; in fact all the squaws of this tribe were good looking, out of the ordinary, but I had other notions just then and did not want to get married under such circumstances, but for prudence sake I seemed to enter into their plans, but at the same time keeping a sharp lookout for a chance to escape.

I noted where the Indians kept their horses at night, even picking out the handsome and fleet Indian pony which I meant to use should opportunity occur, and I seemed to fall in with the Indians' plans and seemed to them so contented that they gave me more and more freedom and relaxed the strict watch they had kept on me, and finally in about thirty days from the time of my capture my opportunity arrived.

My wounds were now nearly well, and gave me no trouble. It was a dark, cloudy night, and the Indians, grown careless in their fancied security, had relaxed their watchfulness. After they had all thrown themselves on the ground and the quiet of the camp proclaimed them all asleep I got up and crawling on my hands and knees, using the greatest caution for fear of making a noise, I crawled about 250 yards to where the horses were picketed, and going to the Indian pony I had already picked out I slipped the skin thong in his mouth which the Indians use for a bridle, one which I had secured and carried in my shirt for some time for this particular purpose, then springing to his back I made for the open prairie in the direction of the home ranch in Texas, one hundred miles away.

All that night I rode as fast as my horse could carry me and the next morning, twelve hours after I left the Indians camp I was safe on the home ranch again. And my joy was without bounds, and such a reception as I received from the boys. They said they were just one day late, and if it hadn't been for a fight they had with some of the same tribe, they would have been to my relief. As it was, they did not expect to ever see me again alive. But that they knew that if the Indians did not kill me, and gave me only half a chance I would get away from them, but now that I was safe home again, nothing mattered much and nothing was too good for me.

It was a mystery to them how I managed to escape death with such wounds as I had received, the marks of which I will carry to my grave and it is as much a mystery to me as the bullet that struck me in the breast just over the heart passed clear through, coming out my back just below the shoulder. Likewise the bullet in my leg passed clear through, then through my horse, killing him.

Those Indians are certainly wonderful doctors, and then I am naturally tough as I carry the marks of fourteen bullet wounds on different parts of my body, most any one of which would be sufficient to kill an ordinary man, but I am not even crippled. It seems to me that if ever a man bore a charm I am the man, as I have had five horses shot from under me and killed, have fought Indians and Mexicans in all sorts of situations, and have been in more tight places than I can number. Yet I have always managed to escape with only the mark of a bullet or knife as a reminder. The fight with the Yellow Dog's tribe is probably the closest call I ever had, and as close a call as I ever want.

The fleet Indian pony which carried me to safety on that memorable hundred mile ride, I kept for about five years. I named him "The Yellow Dog Chief." And he lived on the best the ranch afforded, until his death which occurred in 1881, never having anything to do except an occasional race, as he could run like a deer. I thought too much of him to use him on the trail and he was the especial pet of every one on the home ranch, and for miles around.

I heard afterwards that the Indians pursued me that night for quite a distance, but I had too much the start and besides I had the fastest horse the Indians owned. I have never since met any of my captors of that time. As they knew better than to venture in our neighborhood again. My wound healed nicely, thanks to the good attention the Indians gave me. My captors took everything of value I had on me when captured. My rifle which I especially prized for old associations sake; also my forty fives, saddle and bridle, in fact my whole outfit leaving me only the few clothes I had on at the time.

My comrades did not propose to let this bother me long,

however, because they all chipped in and bought me a new outfit, including the best rifle and revolvers that could be secured, and I had my pick of the ranch horses for another mount. During my short stay with the Indians I learned a great deal about them, their ways of living, sports, dances, and mode of warfare which proved of great benefit to me in after years. The oblong shields they carried were made from tanned buffalo skins and so tough were they made that an arrow would not pierce them although I have seen them shoot an arrow clean through a buffalo. Neither will a bullet pierce them unless the ball hits the shield square on, otherwise it glances off.

All of them were exceedingly expert with the bow and arrow, and they are proud of their skill and are always practicing in an effort to excel each other. This rivalry extends even to the children who are seldom without their bows and arrows.

They named me Buffalo Papoose, and we managed to make our wants known by means of signs. As I was not with them a sufficient length of time to learn their language, I learned from them that I had killed five of their number and wounded three while they were chasing me and in the subsequent fight with my empty gun. The wounded men were hit in many places, but they were brought around all right, the same as I was. After my escape and after I arrived home it was some time before I was again called to active duty, as the boys would not hear of me doing anything resembling work, until I was thoroughly well and rested up. But I soon began to long for my saddle and the range.

And when orders were received at the ranch for two thousand head of cattle, to be delivered at Dodge City, Kansas, I insisted on taking the trail again. It was not with any sense of pride or in bravado that I recount here the fate of the men who have fallen at my hand.

It is a terrible thing to kill a man no matter what the cause. But as I am writing a true history of my life, I cannot leave these facts out. But every man who died at my hands was either seeking my life or died in open warfare, when it was a case of killing or being killed.

The Negro Speaks of Rivers

BY LANGSTON HUGHES

I'VE KNOWN rivers:
I've known rivers ancient as the world and older than the
    flow of human blood in human veins.

My soul has grown deep like the rivers.

I bathed in the Euphrates when dawns were young.
I built my hut near the Congo and it lulled me to sleep.
I looked upon the Nile and raised the pyramids above it.
I heard the singing of the Mississippi when Abe Lincoln went
    down to New Orleans, and I've seen its muddy bosom turn
    all golden in the sunset.

I've known rivers:
Ancient, dusky rivers.

My soul has grown deep like the rivers.

Thank You, M'am

BY LANGSTON HUGHES

SHE WAS a large woman with a large purse that had everything in it but a hammer and nails. It had a long strap, and she carried it slung across her shoulder. It was about eleven o'clock at night, dark, and she was walking alone, when a boy ran up behind her and tried to snatch her purse. The strap broke with the sudden single tug the boy gave it from behind. But the boy's weight and the weight of the purse combined caused him to lose his balance. Instead of taking off full blast as he had hoped, the boy fell on his back on the sidewalk and his legs flew up. The large woman simply turned around and kicked him right square in his blue-jeaned sitter. Then she reached down, picked the boy up by his shirt front, and shook him until his teeth rattled.

After that the woman said, "Pick up my pocketbook, boy, and give it here."

She still held him tightly. But she bent down enough to permit him to stoop and pick up her purse. Then she said, "Now ain't you ashamed of yourself?"

Firmly gripped by his shirt front, the boy said, "Yes'm."

The woman said, "What did you want to do it for?"

The boy said, "I didn't aim to."

She said, "You a lie!"

By that time two or three people passed, stopped, turned to look, and some stood watching.

"If I turn you loose, will you run?" asked the woman.

"Yes'm," said the boy.

"Then I won't turn you loose," said the woman. She did not release him.

"Lady, I'm sorry," whispered the boy.

"Um-hum! Your face is dirty. I got a great mind to wash your face for you. Ain't you got nobody home to tell you to wash your face?"

"No'm," said the boy.

"Then it will get washed this evening," said the large woman, starting up the street, dragging the frightened boy behind her.

He looked as if he were fourteen or fifteen, frail and willow-wild, in tennis shoes and blue jeans.

The woman said, "You ought to be my son. I would teach

you right from wrong. Least I can do right now is to wash your face. Are you hungry?"

"No'm," said the being-dragged boy. "I just want you to turn me loose."

"Was I bothering *you* when I turned that corner?" asked the woman.

"No'm."

"But you put yourself in contact with *me*," said the woman. "If you think that that contact is not going to last awhile, you got another thought coming. When I get through with you, sir, you are going to remember Mrs. Luella Bates Washington Jones."

Sweat popped out on the boy's face and he began to struggle. Mrs. Jones stopped, jerked him around in front of her, put a half nelson about his neck, and continued to drag him up the street. When she got to her door, she dragged the boy inside, down a hall, and into a large kitchenette-furnished room at the rear of the house. She switched on the light and left the door open. The boy could hear other roomers laughing and talking in the large house. Some of their doors were open, too, so he knew he and the woman were not alone. The woman still had him by the neck in the middle of her room.

She said, "What is your name?"

"Roger," answered the boy.

"Then, Roger, you go to that sink and wash your face," said the woman, whereupon she turned him loose—at last. Roger looked at the door—looked at the woman—looked at the door—*and went to the sink.*

"Let the water run until it gets warm," she said. "Here's a clean towel."

"You gonna take me to jail?" asked the boy, bending over the sink.

"Not with that face, I would not take you nowhere," said

the woman. "Here I am trying to get home to cook me a bite to eat, and you snatch my pocketbook! Maybe you ain't been to your supper either, late as it be. Have you?"

"There's nobody home at my house," said the boy.

"Then we'll eat," said the woman. "I believe you're hungry—or been hungry—to try to snatch my pocketbook!"

"I want a pair of blue suede shoes," said the boy.

"Well, you didn't have to snatch *my* pocketbook to get

some suede shoes," said Mrs. Luella Bates Washington Jones. "You could of asked me."

"M'am?"

The water dripping from his face, the boy looked at her. There was a long pause. A very long pause. After he had dried his face, and not knowing what else to do, dried it again, the boy turned around, wondering what next. The door was open. He could make a dash for it down the hall. He could run, run, run, *run!*

The woman was sitting on the daybed. After a while she

said, "I were young once and I wanted things I could not get."

There was another long pause. The boy's mouth opened. Then he frowned, not knowing he frowned.

The woman said, "Um-hum! You thought I was going to say *but,* didn't you? You thought I was going to say, *but I didn't snatch people's pocketbooks.* Well, I wasn't going to say that." Pause. Silence. "I have done things, too, which I would not tell you, son—neither tell God, if He didn't already know. Everybody's got something in common. So you set down while I fix us something to eat. You might run that comb through your hair so you will look presentable."

In another corner of the room behind a screen was a gas plate and an icebox. Mrs. Jones got up and went behind the screen. The woman did not watch the boy to see if he was going to run now, nor did she watch her purse, which she left behind her on the daybed. But the boy took care to sit on the far side of the room, away from the purse, where he thought she could easily see him out of the corner of her eye if she wanted to. He did not trust the woman *not* to trust him. And he did not want to be mistrusted now.

"Do you need somebody to go to the store," asked the boy, "maybe to get some milk or something?"

"Don't believe I do," said the woman, "unless you just want sweet milk yourself. I was going to make cocoa out of this canned milk I got here."

"That will be fine," said the boy.

She heated some lima beans and ham she had in the icebox, made the cocoa, and set the table. The woman did not ask the boy anything about where he lived, or his folks, or anything else that would embarrass him. Instead, as they ate, she told him about her job in a hotel beauty shop that stayed open late, what the work was like, and how all kinds of women came in and out, blondes, redheads, and Spanish. Then she cut him a half of her ten-cent cake.

"Eat some more, son," she said.

When they were finished eating, she got up and said, "Now here, take this ten dollars and buy yourself some blue suede shoes. And next time, do not make the mistake of latching onto *my* pocketbook *nor nobody else's*—because shoes got by devilish ways will burn your feet. I got to get my rest now. But from here on in, son, I hope you will behave yourself."

She led him down the hall to the front door and opened it. "Good night! Behave yourself, boy!" she said, looking out into the street as he went down the steps.

The boy wanted to say something other than, "Thank you, m'am," to Mrs. Luella Bates Washington Jones, but although his lips moved, he couldn't even say that as he turned at the foot of the barren stoop and looked up at the large woman in the door. Then she shut the door.

Papau-New Guinea

Introduction

In the South Pacific lies New Guinea, the second largest island in the world. This huge land mass, 1,500 miles long, is divided into three countries. The western one-half of the island comprises Netherlands New Guinea. Papua is the southeast one-quarter of the island, while New Guinea is the northeast one-quarter; both are controlled by Australia. Each of the territories of Papua and New Guinea is about the size of Oregon.

The geography of New Guinea ranges from mountains 16,000 feet high to swampy plains and thick forests in which it rains almost constantly. Since it is nearly impossible to travel through some of the wetter areas, Papua and New Guinea have never been completely explored. Some regions have been so isolated since men have been on the earth that people there have had no contact with the world outside.

While the territories of Papua-New Guinea are some of the least developed parts of the world, the entire island is rich in copra, cocoa, rubber, coffee, nutmeg, oil, and gold. As long as 1,000 years ago, a few outsiders traveled to New Guinea to get these valuable products.

It is important to keep in mind that, although the New Guineans and Papuans are Third World people, they come from a different racial stock from black Africans, West Indians, and Americans.

The more than two million people who live in the two territories speak hundreds of different languages. Because each language group tends to be a small, isolated community, the islanders have always been a scattered people. Therefore, it has generally been easy for outsiders to take advantage of them.

New Guinea is thick with jungle and remains almost totally undeveloped. There are a few large communities such as Port Moresby, but most people dwell in hundreds of small towns and villages. This will almost certainly change as more of the people in New Guinea leave their villages to work in the mines and other infant industries.

This time of change and wider association is illustrated by the life story of Albert Maori Kiki. "A Visit to Orokolo" tells of his trip to a coastal village and of his contact with the world outside his home. In his book, *Kiki: Ten Thousand Years in a Lifetime*, Mr. Kiki explains how he came from a nomadic tribe which still hunts with bows and arrows. When he grew up, he traveled to the island of Fiji to study medicine, and then worked on the island of Buka for a year. He has now returned home to work among his people as a medical man and a political leader.

More and more New Guineans and Papuans are leaving their villages to attend universities. George Tuke, such a young man, is a student at the University of Papua-New Guinea. His poem, "The Eagle," pictures the great soaring bird looking down on the world "As tiny as a coconut fruit."

"Song of a Hen," like "The Eagle," is interesting as it shows a poet imagining the thoughts of one of nature's creatures. In "Song of a Hen" the original Buin language title is "Tee Kuntee," words which are intended to imitate the cry of a hen. Women in southern Bougainville (a part of the territory of New Guinea) sing this song at festivals.

"The Cycle of A'Aisa" is an ancient Mekeo song from Allan Natachee's Papuan village. It is a hymn of praise for Aia, the Creator of earth and all life. To the singer, the God Aia is all-powerful and everywhere.

In the religious beliefs of many peoples around the world we often read of a first man who brings forth the population of the earth. Often these creators have qualities of both human beings and animals. In the story of "How Man Began," for instance, there is the possum man who grows from the bones of a possum, then turns into a tree. When the first man chops down this tree many people magically emerge from it. Perhaps the most interesting thing about this story is how aimless and accidental the action seems to be: the eating of the possum in the first place, the casual discarding of the bones, and so on. This emphasis on the accidental aspect of creation is common in world mythology.

Dugari is another "first man" who, with the help of Gatumo, the wind, creates the original woman. "The First Woman" is an extremely rich and beautiful account of Dugari's loneliness. Dugari is fascinated by and attracted to the beauties and dangers of nature: the palm tree, the taro-lily, the snake, the octopus, the dog, the ants. Finally, the voice of the wind instructs Dugari to combine all of these things into one in order to create woman. When Dugari insists on adding one more element, the story takes a turn which may seem humorous to men, but not to women.

Another story of how things came to be, "Why the Sun and Moon Are in the Sky," explains how part of our universe came about. Notice that the sun and moon are given human characteristics; they are described as "brother and sister." Clearly, it is always easier for a man to understand the mysteries of nature by beginning with himself. So it happens here that man explains the puzzle of existence by beginning with human qualities, by viewing the sun and moon as similar to mankind—able to feel hungry, sad, and lonely.

The First Woman

THERE WAS a man named Dugari, long ago, who lived in a cave on the edge of a valley high up on the great hill which is called Baugora. The valley was well sheltered and had some good soil where *taitu* grew well. A big stream ran through the valley, falling over rocky walls and foaming between big black boulders; but making deep, still pools in some places, where Dugari used to catch fish, and to swim on very hot days.

But Dugari was very lonely. There was nobody else in the valley, and he never went far away from it because the world was full of spirits and sorcery in those days, and he could not tell what might happen to him if he went among them. There were no spirits in his valley, probably because it was too lonely for them.

So Dugari believed that he was the only man in the world; and perhaps he was, though it was so long ago that nobody can tell.

Anyhow, as I said before, he was very lonely. Sometimes he would sit under a palm tree and talk to it. He loved the shade of the palm, and sometimes it seemed to speak to him when the wind blew through it. But he found that the shade would not stay in one place, but moved as the sun travelled on to its setting.

Then he made a friend of the *taro*-lily, because he loved the soft whiteness of its delicate flowers, which used to nod to him when he talked. But he found that the blossoms died after a few days, and lost all their beauty. He talked to Aurama, the black snake, for he admired its shiny litheness and the sinuous grace of its movements; until one day he saw the venom on its long white fangs, and felt a sudden fear of it.

His next attempt at friendship was with a fresh-water octopus that lived among the rocks in one of the still pools. He liked the way its long arms curved round its prey, and the smooth, quick grace of their motion; but one day he tried to caress it, when the arms twined, one after another, round his arm, and he was nearly pulled into the pool. He managed to pull the octopus out of the pool and kill it, and then mourned because he could not watch it any more.

There was a wild dog that came sometimes to his cave, and he admired its quick alertness and the apparent smoothness

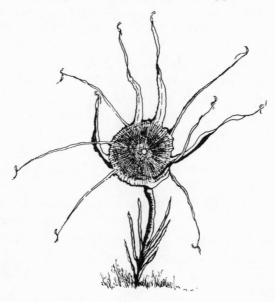

of its coat. He made friendly overtures to it, and gave it scraps of food, so that it came more often, and sometimes approached him when he was out in the forest collecting *taitu* or fishing in the river pools. But one evening, when his back was turned, it seized the fine fish that he had cooked for his evening meal and ran, so that he was angry, and threw stones at it whenever it came afterwards to his cave.

He watched the ants at their work, building huge black mud nests on the trunks of the forest trees. It was wonderful to watch their strength and perseverance. One day he saw them dragging a stick, many hundreds times heavier than themselves, up the tree trunk to the nest. He tried to help them, but as soon as he touched the stick they swarmed on to his hand and arm. All the ants in the colony dropped their loads and hurried to attack him, so that he had to plunge into the river to rid himself of the sting of their bites.

He caught a parrot, and fastened it by one leg to a stick at the mouth of his cave, and was pleased when it called to him as he came home late in the evening; but the parrot's words were only his own words and, though he loved to hear them, he knew that they meant nothing, and that the parrot was not really his friend.

The river was the nearest thing to a friend that he had. Every day he sat beside it and talked to it, and every day it murmured to him in its own language. He loved the sound of it rippling over gravel in the shallow places, singing loudly over and round the boulders, roaring splendidly in the falls. And he loved the sight of it; the mist that rose above the falls and rapids; the swiftly changing lights where it foamed white in the cataracts, and the soft, cool darkness of it in the quiet pools. And at night he used to lie in his cave and listen to its voice below him.

But even the river could not give him the friendship that he sought.

As the years passed he grew more and more lonely until, on a fine bright morning, when every bird in the thick jungle of the valley was calling, and the sun shone warmly even through the morning mist at the mouth of his cave he climbed upon a rocky cliff and stood on a flat limestone shelf from beneath which the river fell, white and thundering, into the head of the valley.

He looked out over the slope on the far side where the uneven carpet of the tree tops fell away from him as far as he could see. There was no motion in them, but only a flash of white now and then, as a cockatoo took wing, circled, and settled again on the branches of a distant tree. But, as he watched, he saw at last a gentle swaying among the green tree tops, and he knew that Gatumo, the south-east wind, was coming. Presently he could hear him moving up the slope, all the trees bending and tossing their heads to him; and a moment later he could feel him, strong and soft and cool, all about him.

"Oh, Dugari," said the wind, "what do you here so early?"

"I am waiting for you, Gatumo," Dugari answered, "for I want to ask advice of you."

"I have not much time to-day," said the wind; "for I have far to go. But tell me your trouble, and I will answer you to-morrow."

"Brother," said Dugari, "I am alone. This valley is good, and I have plenty of food and a good cave, warm and dry. But I have no friend, and I am tired of living by myself. Every morning I go out from my cave and I bring in food. Then I sleep while the sun is high. Afterwards I cook my food and I eat it, and sleep. Every day is the same, and I have no one to be with me."

But before he had finished speaking the south-east wind had passed on, and Dugari returned to his valley.

The next morning he was up on the limestone shelf again,

waiting for the wind to come by. And presently he came.

"Take a palm tree for your friend, Dugari," he said. "For it is strong and tall, and it will give you shelter from the sun at noon. Also it will speak to you when I stir its leaves. This is the best advice that I can give you."

Gatumo, the south-east wind, passed on, and Dugari was disappointed, for he had tried to make a friend of the palm tree without success.

Next day he waited for Gatumo again, and when he came he told him how the palm tree moved its shade.

"Then try the taro-lily," said Gatumo. "It is white and soft and beautiful to look at; and it can nod its head quite as gracefully as the palm." And he hurried on his way.

Each morning Dugari waited for him, and each morning the south-east wind had some new advice to give him; but always he advised something that Dugari had already tried. And Dugari grew more and more unhappy till at last Gatumo took pity on him.

"I will tell you what you must do," said Gatumo thoughtfully; "you must take a leaf of the palm tree and a petal of the lily; the head of a snake and the eye of an octopus; the heart of a dog and the leg of an ant. And you must take as much water as you can carry in your two hands. When the moon is big and high, you must place them in a hollow rock and cover them with ferns. And every morning, when the sun awakes, and at every noon, and at the sleep time of the sun, you must walk round the rock three times and three times and three. And you must say as you walk: 'Comfort and beauty and cunning; patience and loyalty and strength; coolness and music of water; be one and be my friend.' This you must do for three years and three years and three. Now I must go." And he hurried away over the mountains into the north-west.

So Dugari went home. He was very glad to know that he

could make his own friend, but he was not pleased that Gatumo had left out the parrot. All night long he thought about it; and in the morning he went again to his limestone rock and waited for Gatumo.

"Oh, Gatumo," he said, "may I not also put in the tongue of a parrot? For what is the use of waiting so long and working so hard to make what I have already? Palm and lily and snake, octopus and ant, dog and water; I can see them and talk to them at any time. I want a friend who can also talk to me."

Gatumo laughed shortly, for by this time he was a little impatient.

"Put it in if you like, Dugari," he said. "Though I think that if you do you will be sorry. But have it your own way." And he hurried off, growling to himself and snatching petulantly at the stunted shrubs that grew among the limestone rocks.

Dugari sat down and thought about what Gatumo said. He did not want to offend the good-natured south-east wind. But almost beneath his feet, as he sat looking down the valley, the river fell thundering, and the mist that rose from it sparkled with many colours in the early sunlight. Palm trees waved their tops down in the valley, parrots chattering about them. *Taro*-lilies nodded their beautiful heads from among the ferns and crevices in the rock; ants were busily building a new home close beside him. He knew that he could find an octopus in the first of the river pools, and snakes in the damp dead leaves under the trees.

"I have them all," he said to himself; "and yet I am lonely. Yet if I make my own friend he will not leave me, but will stay with me always. I know that I am right, and that speech is the one thing that he must have."

So he went down to his cave and waited day after day until the moon was full. Then he cleaned out a hollow in a rock just outside the mouth of his cave. And he took all the things that Gatumo had told him to take; and when the moon was high he placed them all together in the hollowed rock and covered them with ferns, and lay down to sleep.

Very early in the morning, before the sun was up, he rose and walked nine times round the rock, saying as he walked: "Comfort and beauty and cunning; patience and loyalty and strength; coolness and music and speech; be one, and be my friend."

He did this again at noon and again at sunset, and repeated it day after day. And the months passed, and the years; and at last, early one morning, just as he had finished walking round the rock, he heard a voice from the hollow beneath the ferns; and the ferns were moving a little.

"Let me out; let me out," cried the voice; and the sound of it was harsh, like the voice of a parrot in flight. "Take away this rubbish and let me out. Will you keep me here always?"

He ran to the rock and removed the ferns from over the hollow; and a young woman stepped out of it and on to the floor of the cave.

Dugari stared at her in amazement, for this was the first human being he had seen. She had arms and legs just as he had, but her body was softer and rounder; and she moved with soft grace, like a palm tree in the wind, or like Aurama, the black snake, gliding smoothly through the grass. In Dugari's eyes she was beautiful beyond words; and he stood gazing at her in wonder. But she began to talk as she hurried about the cave; and as she talked his heart grew heavy, for her voice was shrill and harsh.

"Oh, it is like a man," she cried, "to have in his cave such a mess as this. And you care not that I must clean it for you. Men were ever a dirty lot, joying like pigs in mud and rubbish; and indeed and indeed you need women to keep you clean. Bring me water quickly. No, go not, but carry this and this away from here; and stand not like a fool looking at me, lest I tear out your eyes, so angry do you make me. Where is the water that I told you to bring? Stand not like an owl in the daytime, but go, and do my bidding. Go, go, go!" And she stamped with her feet and waved her arms at him, screaming.

So Dugari took a bamboo and brought water from the river and give it to her; and she sprinkled it about the floor of the cave, so that the dust should not rise round her every time that she moved. And still she talked; and Dugari stood and stared in wonder until she sent him out again. She sent him to bring more water, and to bring *taitu* and fish and herbs; and she made him roll away rocks from the mouth of the cave and pull up grass and shrubs till the ground was clear all about it. And all the time she talked without ceasing, till Dugari's head was sore from the noise of it.

At last he went from the cave and wandered down the valley. But soon he longed to hear the woman's voice again, and to see her moving busily about the cave. He went back to her, and she spoke angrily to him for standing about the cave, doing nothing; and at last she threw stones at him, so that he ran from her and sat beside the river.

"Oh, water," he said, "what is this that I have done? For three years and three years and three I waited for her. Almost I quarrelled with my friend Gatumo that she might come to me with speech. And now her speech is so much that I cannot bear it. Why did I not leave her without speech, as Gatumo counselled me? And now, what can I do?"

But the river only laughed at him as it hurried over the pebbles; and the sound of its laughter was very sweet to him. "Ah," he sighed to himself; "if only her voice were like the voice of the water, how perfect she would be!"

At last, when the sun was down, he went back to the cave, fearing her scolding. But she sat by the fire, singing softly to herself. In her hair she wore red blossoms; and she smiled at him, with her small white teeth gleaming in the firelight, so that he looked at her in wonder at her great beauty. And she spoke to him, smiling.

"Come, my friend, and sit with me by the fire and talk with me. Why have you left me so long alone?"

So he sat beside her; and she took food from the fire, and they ate, side by side; and she talked to him with a voice soft and musical as the laughter of the stream over pebbles, and as the breezes in the palm trees. And she looked at him with eyes that were soft and true as the eyes of a dog, but much more beautiful; and she nodded her head gracefully like the flower of the *taro*-lily; and he was well content.

In the morning he woke before the dawn and heard her voice again; but now it was harsh and ugly as before.

"Up, lazy one," she cried. "Will you sleep all the day? Out, to your work, and leave me to mine. For I will work, even though you be stupid and slothful. How you lived before I came I know not, for you do nothing but sit and dream, or sleep, dreaming. Out, useless one! To your work!"

So he went out; and far down the valley he could hear her voice, harsh and angry, as she worked about the cave. Sometimes she called to him, and he ran to her and did her bidding. And all the time she spoke angrily to him, calling him stupid, clumsy, lazy, till he marvelled to learn how useless he was.

But in the evening, when work was done, again she was soft and kind, and her voice was beautiful. And so day after day. But sometimes she was angry in the evening, too; and Dugari sat in the darkness away from the fire, while she shouted at him, her voice harsh like that of a parrot on the wing, so that he longed for the time when she would sleep and be silent. But on such evenings she talked even in her sleep, till Dugari got up silently and left the cave. Then she would call him harshly to come back, and not go wandering idly through the night; so that Dugari was almost mad from the noise of her talking.

At last he felt that he could bear it no longer; and he went up to the limestone rock and called to the south-east wind.

"I am here, Dugari," said the wind. "What do you want of me?"

"Ah, Gatumo!" he cried. "Tell me how I may stop her talk. For all day she talks angrily, and at night I cannot sleep for the noise of it. Tell me how I may take speech away from her, for I can bear it no longer."

And the south-east wind laughed loud and long.

"I told you, Dugari," he said at last, "that you would be wise not to give her speech. Yet you would have it, and for nine years you worked to give it to her. You cannot now take it away. So long as she lives she will talk. Yet there is one thing that I can do for you. I can take you away from her, so that you will see her no more, nor hear her voice again."

"Ah, no, Gatumo," said Dugari at once. "That you shall never do. You have not seen the beauty of her eyes, or the grace of her limbs. Nor have you heard the sound of her voice when she is kind. It is true that she scolds me and curses me. It is true that she throws stones at me, and calls me fool, and idler, and useless one. But she is mine, and I have no other. No, Gatumo. No—no—no. I will *not* go away from her."

The south-east wind laughed as he went on his way; and Dugari returned to his cave.

Why the Sun and Moon Are in the Sky

"Once the sun and the moon were brother and sister. They came up out of the ground in the centre of a certain village. There they lived for a time. They slept in a hole in the ground. During the time the sun slept the moon went wandering about the village. The men of the village caught her and hung her on their spears to light their way through the forest. One of the men fell in love with her beauty. He made a love potion which he placed down in the hole when the moon was asleep there. Then he made a sing-sing.

"The moon woke under the spell of the young man's love charm. She desperately wanted to go to the sing-sing but her

brother, the sun, stopped her. He threatened, "If you go to
the sing-sing I will go away and leave you." The sun then
was hungry so he went off in search of food. The moon wept.
In her great sadness, she jumped into a cooking pot to be
killed. But the pot was cold, so she jumped out and up onto
a door lintel, then onto the roof of a hut. From there she
went up into a betel nut tree, then to a higher tree and so on,
right up into the sky. The sun returned. He missed his sister,
so he went out looking for her. He asked everyone he met if
she had been seen. One of the men told him that she had de-
parted for the sky. He looked up and when he saw her sailing
by, he asked in desperation, "How am I to get up there with
her?" The moon's lover took pity on him and made him a
ladder of rope. Up climbed the sun and joined his sister in
the sky, where they remain to this day."

How Man Began

"A MAN MADE a field and planted potatoes. A possum came and ate them all. The man and his brother came and saw that the possum had eaten all the potatoes. It was sitting in a tree. They pursued it, killed and ate it. They put the bones of the possum in a river and then went home. They slept for two nights, and when they came back they saw that the possum's bones had developed eyes, ears and legs, like a man. They went home again and slept two more nights. Then they returned and looked at the possum. He was now a real man. The possum-man came out of the water and made himself a bow and arrow. He stayed by the river a whole month. The two men from the village returned again to find the possum-man. He stood by the river. They saw him disappear into the water. One of the men went home and told his wife about it. She made a grass belt and grass bracelets for the possum-man. They went down to the river to look for him. There was no possum-man. A large tree had arisen in the place where he had disappeared. A strange sound came from the tree, like the song of many birds. The man cut the tree down with his stone axe. He then cut a big hole in the tree. Men and women came out of the tree. He chopped off some more of the tree and more men and women came out.

He went on chopping and still men and women came out.
They were all singing. All the women wanted a man. They
each caught hold of a man and said: "This man is mine."
The man who had cut down the tree gave them each a name
and told them where to go and live. They all sang as they
went off through the long grass. They built huts. The women
gave birth to children. They grew up—and here we are."

The Eagle

BY GEORGE TUKE

I AM KING of the earth,
I am king of the air,
I am king of the ocean.
Everything is around my throne
Under my powerful wings.
Sunrise to sunset
I look over the world
As a tiny coconut fruit
Floating on a silvery sea.
I know the spirit of the air,
I know the spirit of the earth,
I know the spirit of the ocean.
Everything is beneath my wings
Under my powerful tail.

The Cycle of A'Aisa

ANONYMOUS

WATER all over
all all over
darkness all over
all all over

Aia sitting seated
Aia living alive

Aia sitting seated
sitting forever
Aia living alive
living forever

Aia without beginning
Aia without end

Above the water
Aia has lived
Aia has watched
above the darkness

Aia has lived
Aia has watched

Aia creator of our earth
Aia creator of our home

Creator of earth
creator creating
creator of home
creator creating

By mouth wind of Aia
we were made
by lip wind of Aia
we were made

Eater eating
things all things
things above
things below

Aia lighting alight
lighting our earth
lighting our home

Aia lighting all over
lighting all our earth
Aia lighting all over
lighting all our home

Tee Kuntee

Song of a Hen

NE MARA kaga tugi rakouna
  tee kuntee tee kuntee
ne paakeu tou raga reu?
  tee kuntee tee kuntee
ne tei keruguamonna
  tee kuntee tee kuntee
noke urugito konkogipomo
  tee kuntee tee kuntee

ne mara kaga tugi rakouna
  tee kuntee tee kuntee
ne paakeu tou raga reu?
  tee kuntee tee kuntee
ne tei keruguamonna
  tee kuntee tee kuntee
mara mairogi konkogipomo
  tee kuntee tee kuntee

MY LEGS are thin like the
  casuarina—
why can't I be more like the
  possum?
I am tired

from chasing away the pigs.

My legs are thin like the casuarina—
why can't I be more like the
  the possum?
I am tired

from chasing away the wicked
  dogs.

A Visit to Orokolo

BY ALBERT MAORI KIKI

ONE DAY my uncles came and decorated my mother. They put the large armshells on her, the dogtooth necklace, the waistbands and the anklets. I had never seen her looking so splendid and wondered what had happened. Soon it was explained to me that we were going down to the coast, to my father's village. I was about four or five years old at the time and all I knew about my father was that he sent occasional gifts of sea fish to us.

Shells were the principal ornaments among the Parevavo people and they actually represented our only form of wealth. The shells had to be obtained from the coastal people by exchanging them for magic charms—the only thing we could trade. The coastal people were infinitely richer in food than we were, but they believed that we possessed certain powers—both protective and destructive. The 'power' trade never went on in the open market, but people met secretly in the bush to negotiate. Judging by my mother's appearance that day, my people must have been pretty successful in this business.

It took us four days to reach Orokolo, my father's village, and most of the way one of my uncles carried me on his chest. I was already too old to be slung in a string bag like the smaller children.

My first impression of Orokolo was that it was full of people. Coming from the tiny Parevavo community that wandered through the thick forest with their scanty belongings, Orokolo seemed like a modern metropolis. There, people lived in solid houses, close together, and the place was buzzing with noise and activity. The vast number of pigs roaming about everywhere also astonished me because my mother's people did not keep any tame pigs, whereas in Orokolo the pig population was larger than the human one.

My mother told me later that she felt a wonderful sense of security in Orokolo, where one could sleep without fearing a night attack by the enemy. But to me the experience was altogether disturbing and worrying. At night I missed the humming noises that had lulled me to sleep at home. The formidable sound made by the crickets in the forest was reduced to a feeble chirping there and the cries of the night birds were altogether absent.

To me, the most frightening thing was the sight of the sea, the unbelievable, roaring expanse of water. Throughout that first year in Orokolo I could never be induced to swim in the sea, nor would I enter a boat.

I was terribly proud of my father, who stood out from everyone else in his uniform. The image that remains most clearly in my mind is that of my father standing among men, telling them what to do, or exhorting them, or making peace. He was also a little frightening, with his heavy leather belt and the steel knife stuck in the side—the first of its kind I had ever seen. My father had two grown-up sons who were married, and three younger adopted children, though none as small as myself. The oldest son was called Heni—after my father's 'trade relation' from Porebada, a Motu village some 200 miles further down the coast.

The Motu people went on regular trade expeditions to the Gulf area. They tied three or four canoes together and built a platform across them. These large craft were known as *la-katoi,* and they brought pots and exchanged them for sago. I saw several of these *Hiri* trading expeditions arriving in

Orokolo. The trade was not conducted like common barter, it was carried out with a certain ceremony; and the declarations of friendship that went with it were as important as the exchange of goods itself.

The arrival of the lakatoi in Orokolo was usually a great occasion. The visitors were greeted with singing. The Motu people did not carry their pots to the market, but each went straight to the house of his 'trade relation', with whom his family had been dealing for years and perhaps generations. Heni, the leader of the expedition, went to my father's house. He would hand over all his pots at once to my father, and it was considered bad manners to count them or to ask for a price. To any outsider the transaction might have looked like a gift. But in fact my father was counting the pots carefully and as they were piled up in the house one of his sons was charged with making knots in a piece of string, different knots for different pot sizes and different shapes.

In this way my father assessed the amount of sago he had to give in return, and once again the sago was presented to the trade relation without counting. Often my father would also go into the bush and cut a canoe for Heni, because the lakatoi might need some repairs and replacements after the long journey up the coast. The friendship between my father and Heni was further cemented when my father called his first son Heni, and his friend called his own son Kiki. In fact Motu trade relations were almost considered members of one's own clan. If one of them were to die in Orokolo, we would bury him with full rites, like one of our own people.

I had some difficulty in learning my father's language. For quite a while I kept silent and when I uttered my first sentence it turned out to be a hotchpotch of Orikolo and Parevavo. I have not been allowed to forget this because to this very day, when my sisters want to tease me, they said: *pairake la akea aeve*.[1] And I must confess, that after thirty odd years, I still get a little angry when they do this. I can remember the original occasion very clearly: I had seen two masks walking through the bush and a couple of young men going in front, brushing the cobwebs off the branches lest they touch the masks. I was so excited by this unfamiliar sight that I overcame my initial shyness and uttered my first unsuccessful sentence in the Orokolo language.

In spite of many similar experiences which, I suppose, any child has to suffer in a new and unfamiliar environment, my life on the coast was a happy one. To us, there was unbelievable comfort there. My mother did not have to do any gardening because in Orokolo this is a man's job. The men clear the bush, plant the taro, the bananas and the sweet potatoes, they do all the weeding and the fencing, and the women are only called in to help with the harvest. The sago palms, of course, were planted many generations ago and they need no attention. But the cutting of the trees and the splitting of the trunk are skilled men's jobs, while the women have to pound the sago.

We children played and ran along the beaches. At home I had never known such wide open spaces, such flat ground for running. I was as good as any child there with my little bows and arrows, but there were many new games to learn. By far the most popular and interesting of these was a kind of hockey game that was played with bent sticks of cane and the hard, round Koae seed that served as a ball. Boys and girls played this game, but unlike the European game there were no goals. The object of the game was to drive the other party of players as far east or west as we could.

[1] The first three words are Orokolo, the fourth Parevavo. The words mean 'Broom up there in the sky!' A coconut-frond broom was used to brush off the cobwebs.

We usually played against a neighbouring village and when we were lucky we would drive them miles along the beach far beyond their village and the game would only stop when the sun set. The boys were in the forefront of the game, hitting the ball with their sticks. But the girls had the privilege of being allowed to catch the ball with their hands. When they did, everyone had to stand still and allow the girl a kind of free kick, and they knew how to hit it hard with their sticks.

In Orokolo the women spend much of their time weaving nets and fishing in the shallow waters. The men catch the bigger fish and go out in canoes at night. There is a long thin fish with a pointed nose called *hariha,* which is attracted by the light that is carried on the boats. This fish was plentiful off the coast in Orokolo and most of the men went out after it. But only a few people knew how to catch young sharks. My father was one of these. No hook was used, but a double loop which was let down deep into the water. As bait, two bits of flesh from a water snake and too small shiny shells were tied to the loop. The sharks would be attracted to the shells from a distance, thinking they were fish. Once they put their heads through the noose they could not retreat, because their gills were caught in it.

The loop is made from the rough bark of the *oro* tree (which has given its name to Orokolo) and by the time the shark is pulled up, it is dead. Often two of them are caught together. Hundreds of small sharks would be caught in this manner to be eaten. Our people did not seem to bother about the large man-eating sharks. They never hunted them, and the sharks in turn seemed to leave us alone. During all the years I lived in Orokolo, I cannot remember a single case of a man being taken by a shark.

There were other fish that could not be caught by just anyone because they belonged to a certain clan. The fish known as *larovea* for example belonged to my father's people. There was a carved image of this fish in my father's house and when the season came for catching *larovea* my father's clan would make a feast and then go to the sea and put the wooden fish into the water. This ritual was intended to attract the fish and usually they came in great swarms. But if *larovea* went into the net of a man who did not belong to my father's clan he would have to throw them back into the water. Only my father's people were allowed to catch them but they could not eat them.

All the fish they caught were distributed among the other people of the village. Though my father's clan could never keep or eat the *larovea* fish, they kept all other fish they caught. They were not given anything directly in exchange. But there is so much exchange of food going on in Orokolo that the people do not bother even to have a market. When a man has a big catch of fish or a large yam harvest, he will automatically distribute some of the food to neighbours, friends, and relatives.

My father told me the following story to explain his relationship to fish:

Lalovea used to be a man and he lived under the mountain. He was an ugly man, so he decided to make a hole under the mountain and stay there. He was a feeble man who could not work. So he used to go out and steal his food. When the people found out about it they tabooed their gardens. They made signs (by knotting ray grass) saying that he was a woman, unable to make his garden, that he was a thief, that he was a beggar. Then Lalovea was ashamed and he went and stayed under the water. When the people saw him sitting under the water he said to them: 'Now you will find it difficult to catch me. You will have to look for me. You will have to fence me in. You must say my name: but if you say the wrong words, I will never come to you.'

Lalovea is the name that is known to everybody. But we alone have the secret name, that is why we alone are allowed to catch him.

Other fish were related to other clans. The fish called
Maria for example belonged to the Kauri clan and they tell
this story about it:

Maria was the youngest son of Molara, and Molara kept
him in the house until one day Maria died. But Molara was
so fond of him that he did not want to bury him. So he dried
the body and smoked it until it became very small. Then he
carried him around under his armpit wherever he went. So
Maria stayed with his father even though he was dead.
Though Maria was dead, he began to grow under Molara's
arm. People soon began to notice that Molara's left shoulder
drooped while his right shoulder turned up. In the end Molara was unable to carry the weight and so he went and put
his son into the Miaru river. Every day he visited him and
fed him until the son grew up and produced other Marias.

When people want to catch Maria they must belong to this
Kauri clan. Someone must go out into the water and pretend
to be Molara. He must identify himself with Molara's secret
name. He can then call out and ask Maria to come and help
him.

Thus much of our fishing activity was bound up with religious ritual and ancestor worship. But the most sacred activity was the planting of yams. Yam planting was not an individ-
ual's business. It had to be done communally because it is a
very sacred plant. There is a special kind of priest known as
Hi Haela—the string man—who must go onto the land first,
alone, and drive out the evil spirits. This is done by cutting
the vines, the wild creepers, which are supposed to be the
magic strings by which evil spirits travel to the earth.

The concept of the magic string is widespread in Orokolo.
It is believed, for example, that the leader of any clan can
physically remove himself to the clan's place of origin within

seconds by travelling on this magic string that will eternally connect him to his origin, rather like a spiritual navel cord.

We stayed in Orokolo for about a year, and then returned to my mother's village. Our last homestead had of course been deserted by this time and our people had moved on. But my mother found no difficulty in tracing them for the young men had marked the path with signs cut on trees or knots tied to shrubs. In our territory each village had its own sign language and strangers coming across these were well advised to keep out of the way because anybody seen following them might be suspected of being an enemy and killed instantly.

This was the first occasion since I was born that my father visited my mother's village. He was now retired as a village constable and he lived with us for some time. I spent several more years in my mother's village and I was about ten or eleven years old when I descended once more to Orokolo. This time I was sent for because I had become old enough to be initiated in my father's community and go through the various *eravo* houses. I had already gone through the initiation in my mother's village, which takes place at an earlier age.

Now I was to face the much more elaborate and complicated ritual of Orokolo. Years were taken up in this activity and I never returned to live at home for any length of time. And thus it happened that in spite of all the lengthy preparation I had been given, and in spite of all the promises I had to make in the *Kapa* bush, I never did prove my manhood by killing a man, and somebody else had to carry out the 'payback' for my dead uncle, which was considered my own duty and privilege in Parevavo.

Acknowledgments

We wish to acknowledge our gratitude for permission to publish the following:

"Wrestling in Iboland," "Breaking a Kola Nut," and "Burial of a Titled Man" from *The Way We Lived* by Rems Nna Umeasiegbu. © 1969. Reprinted by permission of Heinemann Educational Books Ltd.

"Joseph the Zulu" from *Tell Freedom* by Peter Abrahams. © 1954. Reprinted by permission of John Farquharson Ltd. and Alfred A. Knopf, Inc.

"Visit to the Village" from *The Dark Child* by Camara Laye. Translated by James Kirkup. © 1955. Reprinted by permission of Collins Publishers and Farrar, Straus & Giroux, Inc.

"How the Milky Way Came to Be" from *African Folk Tales* by Charlotte and Wolf Leslau. © 1963. Reprinted by permission of Peter Pauper Press.

"Nyangara, the Python" from *The Lion on the Path and Other African Stories* by Hugh Tracey. © 1968. Reprinted by permission of Routledge & Kegan Paul Ltd., and Praeger Publishers, Inc.

"People Can't Be Made From Iron" from *The Baganda: An Account of Their Native Customs and Beliefs* by John Roscoe. © 1911. Reprinted by permission of Macmillan, London and Basingstoke.

"Why the Spider Has a Small Head" from *Akar-Ashanti Folk-Tales* by R. S. Rattray. © 1930. Reprinted by permission of the Clarendon Press, Oxford.

"Leopard Hunt" from *I Was a Savage* by Prince Modupe, copyright, 1957 by Harcourt Brace Jovanovich, Inc., and reprinted with their permission.

"Song of an Unlucky Man" from *Umbundu: Folk Tales From Angola* by Merlin Ennis. Copyright © 1962 by Merlin Ennis. Reprinted by permission of Beacon Press.

"My Wish" from *Talent For Tomorrow* by Philomena Kassewa Kaka. © 1966. Reprinted by permission of Ghana Publishing Corp., Accra.

"Living in the Forest." Edited by Miguel Barnet, and translated by Jocasta Innes. © 1968. Reprinted from *The Autobiography of a Runaway Slave* by Estaban Montejo, by permission of The Bodley Head Limited, London and Pantheon Books.

"The Barracuda" from The *Shark Hunters* by Andrew Salkey. © 1966. Reprinted by permission of Thomas Nelson & Sons Limited.

"Anansi and Turtle and Pigeon" from *Anansi the Spider Man* by Philip Sherlock. © 1966. Reprinted by permission of Macmillan, London and Basingstoke.

"Makonaima Returns" from *Makonaima Returns* by Henry W. Josiah. © 1966. Reprinted by permission of the author.

THIS BOOK IS SET IN 11 POINT BASKER-
VILLE TYPE WITH GOUDY LIGHT DISPLAY.
IT IS PRINTED ON 80 POUND EGGSHELL
PAPER AND HAS A REINFORCED BINDING
OF COLUMBIA BAYSIDE CLOTH. IT WAS
COMPOSED, PRINTED AND BOUND BY THE
COLONIAL PRESS INC.

DESIGNED BY BARBARA KOHN ISAAC